The

Gettysburg

Ghost

By

Philip N. Rogone

Caring Creations Publishing
7245 Jenkins Ave.
Hesperia, CA 92345

The Gettysburg Ghost

By

Philip N. Rogone

Kind words from some readers:

"I caught myself laughing and crying. Obviously your book has the power to suck the reader in. As of right now tears are in my eyes because of the love you managed to trap on paper…"

Ericka R.

"I truly enjoyed your story of the Gettysburg Ghost. I'm sad it's over. It has a wonderful ending. I enjoyed so much having my husband read it to me every night. I almost want him to re-read it to me…."

Elise G.

"I bought your book while you were at a signing in Gettysburg. It took me 2 days to finish your book. I loved it and am so glad I purchased it that day. I hope you continue with your Civil War writing…"

Renee G.J.

"I just finished your book 'The Gettysburg Ghost.' It was a delightful love story. Once I started it I could barely put it down until I finished it in three short days. Now I am going to share it with my mother."

Beverly S.

"It is a wonderful book. Thank you for sharing it with me. It was so romantic and sad and happy and mushy. I hope to find love like that someday. It was exactly what I needed on a long Sunday afternoon, as well as a good cry, very cleansing...   Karilynn Clear Channel Radio

"Your clever interweaving of several love stories which spanned as many generations was written with warmth and sensitivity. Thank you for bringing us this memorable story."   Adrienne J.

"What a lovely, haunting story with a touching message...a real treasure find! I will keep this book in a special place in my library among my favorite novels. Thanks so much for sharing your gift of storytelling..."   Catherine L.

"...I absolutely loved it! I laughed and cried. I cried tears of sadness and tears of joy. You are an amazing creator. Your characters were sincere and diverse.   Wanda P.

For information on how individual consumers can place orders please go to **www.caringcreations.com**.

The

Gettysburg Ghost

A Novel By

Philip N. Rogone

Caring Creations Publishers
Hesperia, California 92345

Philip N. Rogone

The Gettysburg Ghost

Copyright © 2003 by Philip N. Rogone & Kenneth S. Croteau
Published by Caring Creations Publishing
Hesperia, California 92345

Lyrics in this text
"They'll Never Believe Me."(Kern-Rourke) from The Girl from Utah 1912
"New York, New York" (Ebb-Kander)
"More" the theme from "Mondo Cane" (Newell-Ortolani)
"Where the Boys Are" (Greenfield-Sedaka)
"Looking for the Right One" (Bishop)
"Can't Take My Eyes Off of You" (Gaudio-Crewe)
"You Are" (Richie-Richie)

Excerpt from "The Prophet" by Kahlil Gibran

Library of Congress Control Number: 2004115583

ISBN 0-9725143-0-9

Text editing by Lynea Search
Cover design by The Rogue
Photo by Terry L. Whittington
Wet Plate photographer

SECOND EDITION September 2006

This book is dedicated to my Mother,

Maria Rogone

Who taught me how to love unconditionally
Who said that success comes to those who
persevere regardless of the obstacles
And who told me to always follow my dreams.

"Ti Amo Mama"

Love in all its agony is still music to the soul.

The Rogue

Prologue

Late June 1863...

As the sun was finalizing its daily journey toward tomorrow, a wounded, exhausted officer covered with dirt and blood, slowly led his chestnut steed across what used to be rich Pennsylvanian farmland. It had only recently become a graveyard. He was surrounded on all sides by the remains of boys and young men alike, in tattered blue and gray uniforms, who just weeks before had been plowing fields and planning their lives—men who would never again see a sunrise or the ones they loved. They had been called up for service, on one side to preserve the union, and on the other to stand up for state's rights. All had died for those ideals.

The officer stood helpless over their bodies, holding back his tears from his troops' view. Then he looked down and rubbed his blood-soaked leg, the assault of metal on man and the horrible results it created. He fought feverishly to avert an overwhelming flow of emotion as he contemplated his personal losses and the utter futility of the war. He felt drawn toward his tent and the small portable field desk, in order to write to his beloved Sarah Elizabeth McKee. If for only a brief time, he knew, this would allow him to escape the hellish reality outside.

As he looked back, he saw bodies being carried to a temporary morgue, where their belongings would be gathered up and their names recorded in a book that was growing larger each day. He would write to the loved ones of those who had just made the ultimate sacrifice. But his few words would be insufficient to describe the loss, the sacrifice, and the honor in which they died. Finally, he would sign his name in a ledger next to those of his young heroes. This would ensure that the personal effects made it home to the soldier's next of kin.

Once out of view of his men, his pent-up emotions made their way to the surface. He wept bitterly for the horrible waste of life and for his country, which was now fighting against itself.

Captain Daniel Sutherland was 28 years old, and a graduate from Harvard University. He had been able to sense the rumbling of war drums as opposing political views were creating a severance of ideologies. He volunteered for the Union militia and was quickly commissioned a second lieutenant. After his unit was activated, his wisdom and his maturity, as well as his skills as a strategist, moved him through the ranks faster than his younger counterparts. Despite his relative youth, he was regarded as somewhat of a father figure by his troops, who turned to him often with concerns of the heart, and questions about the struggle that faced them. He always seemed to know what to say to dispel their fears. But, alone in his transient fortress of solitude, he needed to turn his own worried heart to his pen, to take solace in the wonder that was Sarah Elizabeth McKee.

His letter read:

My beloved Sarah,

I am compelled to begin this correspondence with a heavy heart, as I have received not a word from you in these past three months. There are so many things that were left unsaid with my departure from you, and I fear if I do not take this time to express them, they might forever be lost.

The battles of late have been more ferocious and destructive, each day bringing more casualties than the day before. Today, all around me lie the broken bodies of honorable men, who paid, too often with their lives, for the chance to reunite our country. As much as I am sure that you know my love for you, know also that the only circumstance that has taken me away from you is my loyalty to our country. This dream of our forefathers is on the brink of destruction, and it is my duty and my solemn trust to preserve their legacy. I will avoid any further mention of this day, as there are other important thoughts I must send to you.

Imagine all the good feelings you have ever known in your heart and then magnify them by a hundred and they would still not measure up to how much I adore you, my darling. I recall often the first instant my eyes beheld your face and I thank God that He has allowed me to memorize it, so that I can recall its loveliness in my moments of deepest despair.

If my destiny is to return home, then the day that I have you in my embrace again shall also be our wedding day. I long so much for you to be my wife and to have you become the mother of my children. However, if this is to be my last contact with you, there are apologies to be made.

My dearest Sarah, if there were times when I hurt you, I am forever sorry, for I have known only love for you in my heart and would never cause you pain intentionally. If my occasional silences have made you fearful of rejection, your fears were unfounded, for they were due only to my own feelings of inadequacy. If you saw me gaze on other women in your presence, it was only to appreciate you the more, for there is no one in the world like you. I will not, however, apologize for our last night together, for it has given me the strength to endure the horrors of war and the senseless destruction of human life.

You see, my Sarah, you are the nourishment that sustains me, the spring that quenches my thirst, and the desire that must be fulfilled. I love you, my darling, with all my heart.

I am unsure what is in God's plan for us. If our Lord chooses to take me in the days ahead, then I suppose that would be His will, but look not to the glorious heavens above for me, as I shall remain close by. Instead, my darling, look for me in the summer wind that surrounds you, for I will be there embracing you as the warm wind brushes your hair.

Listen to the crackling fire as it burns brightly in your hearth, for it will be my passion for you, heating your very soul as you attempt to go through the wintry nights without me.

Look up when the spring rain falls, for it will be my lips delivering soft, wet kisses like the gentle passionate kisses of our last night together.

Finally, when your soft, blue eyes have grown weak through countless seasons in the sun, your strawberry blond hair has turned to soft silver silk lying gently across your shoulders, and the pages of my letters become too hard to read ... I will be there. And when eternity finds you and you draw your last earthly breath, fear not your departure from this world ... for I will be beside you and I will catch you as you fall.

Until forever

Daniel Sutherland

Daniel was about ready to seal his letter when he once more stared out beyond the flap of his tent. As the fog rolled in across the bloody valley, his eyes again focused on the dying, the sea of severed young lives, and he hastily added the following line …

Post Script: War has only taught me how very fragile we all are.

He lowered his pen just as his friend, company doctor Major James Muny, arrived at his tent to demand that he get to the hospital so they could clean and dress his wounded limb.

"Dan, you don't want to lose your leg today ... do you?" The doctor stood in the doorway and stared impatiently at the Captain with a look of intolerance. Getting no response he turned, kicking the air as he headed back toward the makeshift hospital. Daniel looked down at his leg and knew his friend was right.

The heavy fog was becoming a moist blanket covering the scene of military death as Daniel slowly limped through the fog toward the hospital.

June 1999

Chapter One

The thick fog made it virtually impossible to see as Barry Landers' Pathfinder thundered down the dark coastal highway. The evening out was not going as planned. He was also confused, angry, and unsure of what to say next. Finally he blurted out, "I can't talk with that music going!" His hand reached down and shut the radio off.

His lovely passenger had been waiting anxiously for their conversation to resume. "What's on your mind, Barry?" questioned Lindy Dennison.

"I want to know why I feel like I'm the only one who gives a damn about this relationship," Barry demanded.

There was a brief moment of silence.

"Well, Barry, you *are* the only one who cares about this relationship," she replied sharply, then continued nervously, without stopping to catch her breath. "Four years ago when you swept me off my feet, I cared deeply for you, and what was important to you … but, with each date and weekend, I have slowly come to realize that I was important to you only as long as it was *your* needs that were being met. My needs, though I mentioned them repeatedly, never seemed to sink into that egocentric head of yours."

As she fought to hold back the tears, Lindy pressed on boldly, "When I told you about my seven years together with John, I assumed you understood my pain when he said goodbye so abruptly. I know I told you how much I thought I loved him. I know I told you I thought we would be together forever. So when he said he didn't want to stay together anymore, I was devastated. I thought I could never feel again, and wasn't even sure I would want to. I

7

promised myself I would never set myself up to get hurt again."

Barry cut in defensively. "Are you saying I hurt you?"

"No, Barry, I seem to be able to do that all by myself," Lindy answered sadly. "I wanted to be really loved so much that I allowed myself to believe that my relationship with John and your affection for me...were love. In your mind I know you think you love me, but the kind of love I need should take my breath away. It should express itself by a man's wanting to hold me in public regardless of who's around. It should feel like butterflies are floating around inside my stomach whenever he walks into a room—just like he should feel for me. He should propose with a ring of promise, and he should never want either of us to ever be alone again. But I see now that instead I've allowed myself to set my aspirations too low, and to settle for less in matters of the heart—and that isn't John's fault and it's not your fault ... it's mine."

"Are you telling me you want to get married? Okay, then we'll get married," Barry responded feeling both guilty and frustrated as he pulled into Lindy's driveway.

She reached over and kissed his cheek. "Barry, I will probably always care for you, but not enough to marry you. I hope we will always be friends. But I cannot do this anymore." Barry sat stunned as she quickly got out of the car, her emotions on the brink of imploding.

On April the first, Lindy Dennison turned 26 years old. She was as beautiful as a liquid amber tree in early autumn. Her figure was slender but rounded in the right places. Her large almond shaped eyes were a soft, peaceful blue, and they sparkled when she smiled. She had full lips that could pout any man into submission, though she used that pout sparingly. Her hair was a strawberry blond, wavy cascade that always looked marvelous, even when wind blown. She had all that, plus a cute nose that turned up ever so slightly. While most women spent hours in front of their mirror in order to look good, she could forget to take the time and still look about as good as a model on a magazine cover.

Lindy also possessed a personal integrity that would not allow her to take advantage of a situation just because of her physical attributes. Her personality was well suited to her position as a sales representative for a medical supply company; as her territory grew, so did her reputation as the kind of woman who could get the job done and get it done with a great smile. She was persuasive without being pushy, a delicate combination in the sales industry.

She met Barry Landers, M.D., while she was in-servicing a small group of neonatal intensive care nurses on how to use a new product called the Bili-Bonnet, a phototherapy mask used to protect an infant's eyes from ultra-violet lights. After the orientation, the handsome doctor approached Lindy. Barry had really poured on the charm, and since it had been quite a while since Lindy had dated, she agreed to a dinner date. But she also remembered her promise to herself never to get hurt again. Thus it was, with feelings well under control, that she began seeing Barry regularly.

Lindy found after a time that she just couldn't be herself around Barry. She never felt at ease. She wouldn't let herself be spontaneous for fear of his reprisals. He liked her to always be in control of her feelings. He also hated her drawing attention to the two of them in public; even holding hands on the street was taboo. So the walls that she had so carefully constructed years before stayed very much in place. Meanwhile she kept telling herself that Barry was a great guy.

Now she found herself at the end of this long-term affair and she couldn't remember at what point she had sold herself out. But after four years and a lot of expended energy, Lindy was sure in her heart that Barry was definitely *not* the man of her dreams. Indeed, at this point in her life, she was beginning to think that man might not even exist.

Lindy scooped up her big, black, longhaired cat Theodore, squeezing him tightly with her embrace. A few tears dropped onto his furry coat before she went over to the answering machine. She hit the play button, noticing the light flashing. Immediately, a voice that she had loved since childhood chanted a lyrical hello and salutations from The Big Apple. She listened as she wiped the tears from her eyes and began dialing before the message ended.

"Janey," she squealed into the phone. "You always know when I need to talk to you! Are you sure you're not a witch?"

Jane Doe, her best friend since her sophomore year of high school, answered, "Of course, I am! How else could I have known that you needed to talk to me? Do you need to talk to me, Lin?"

Lindy laughed through her tears, then and told Jane what had happened. "I broke up with Barry. It just wasn't working out between us; I know you know what I mean."

Jane let her finish. "He was a wonderful guy. He just wasn't *your* wonderful guy. Well, I guess I can stop lighting candles at the church. It was costing me a fortune." There was a bit of sarcasm in her voice.

"Stop it, Jane," Lindy scolded her friend. "He is a nice guy."

"Yes, he is," Jane, answered, adding under her breath, "As long as he gets his way."

Lindy missed Jane's added comment and Jane was just as glad, because she didn't want Lindy spending the rest of their conversation defending the 'nice guy.' Jane quickly changed the subject: "I called to remind you as I do every year, my dearest friend in all the world, that I will be going to Gettysburg for the Civil War reenactment, and as I do each and every year, I am begging you to join me," Jane said in her kindest voice, waiting patiently for the ritual, "I can't" from Lindy, which she had come to expect.

There was a moment of silence, and then much to Jane's surprise Lindy answered casually, "Why not?"

She caught her friend off guard in her matter-of-fact tone. Jane wasn't quite ready for that answer. For what seemed to Lindy the very first time in all the years she had known her, Jane was speechless. Finally she spoke. "I can't believe this ... you're not teasing me, are you?"

"No, I'm not," assured her friend, "I'll just have to make a few phone calls so I can get away for a week..." She paused suddenly to ask, "Is a week long enough?"

"Can you stay for two weeks? That way we can go to Gettysburg, and then afterwards I can give you the grand tour of New York—you know, Empire State Building, Statue of Liberty, and of course a Broadway show."

"Okay," replied Lindy, "I'll get two weeks off work. I haven't taken a real vacation in the past two years, so I have the vacation time coming." She paused for a moment then said, "Yes, two weeks is no problem at all."

Jane shouted back happily, "That's awesome!"

Both girls' voices rose in excitement as questions of what to bring, weather reports, things to see and things to do made their way into a conversation filled with much happy giggling. "But why are you finally saying yes?" Jane questioned through the excitement.

"Because," said her friend, "I've spent my last eleven years going in one, and only one, direction, and it has taken me all the way to *nowhere*. Perhaps my destiny can't be charted as I always thought it could be. Maybe I should let God take over; since in my effort to control absolutely everything in my life, I've learned that most things are outside my control anyway. So I figure, heck, I might as well have some fun along the way."

Then Lindy's tone changed. "You know, Jane, this week I read a book called *The Prophet*. Have you ever read it?"

Jane gave her a quick affirmative.

"It's really been enlightening. There's one line in it that says...wait, let me read it to you, because I don't want to mess it up." There was a silence and then the rustling of pages. "Here it is. Listen ... *'Think not you can direct the course of love, for love if it finds you worthy, directs your course.'* I love that line, and I decided that right about now that sounds like pretty good advice for me."

The girls giggled some more and broke into their own rendition of *New York, New York*.

♪*Start spreading the news ... ♫ I'm leaving today. ♪ I'm gonna make a brand new start of it, in old New York ... ♫.*"

The next day Lindy went to her boss Jeffrey Lyons and requested the time off. He looked at her in disbelief, then said, "I wondered when you were ever going to take a real vacation."

She smiled at him and then told him about Barry. "You told me this was bound to happen, Jeff...I just couldn't keep kidding myself. He just wasn't the one." She paused for a moment, and then wondered aloud, "Maybe this trip isn't such a good idea right now..."

"Are you kidding, Lin? After a break-up that's all the more reason to get away. It'll help you clear your head. It's always worked for me," her supervisor said knowingly with a smile. Then he got back to business. "Why don't you call Rick Dunhill and get him acquainted with your hospitals. I think he's ready to get his feet wet, and I'd rather he learned from you than from anyone else."

"Thanks Boss." She smiled her reply.

The next morning, she called Rick and had him meet her at one of her largest hospitals in Loma Linda. She made contact with the nurse manager and introduced her temporary replacement. Rick was eager to give a handshake and announce enthusiastically, "If there's anything you need, anything at all, just call 24 hours a day. I don't care when." Lindy glanced over at the nurse as Rick finished speaking. Then Lindy told her, "You'll be well taken care of while I'm away and not to worry because I'll be back before you know it."

Everywhere she went the people she had come to know told her how glad they were that she was finally taking a vacation. She was quite surprised to learn that so many friends were familiar with the Gettysburg reenactment ceremonies that she described.

Later that afternoon she packed up all of Barry's clothes and personal things that he'd left at her place. Then she called him to tell him she would be coming by. Once there, they exchanged a few words.

Barry, as usual, was feeling sorry for himself because things hadn't gone his way. There was sarcasm in his voice. "So, Ms. Independent, what's your next move?" he whined.

She told him she was going to New York and then to Gettysburg with Jane.

He said, "Sounds like a crazy thing to do right now ... doesn't it?" Barry was always trying to make her unsure of herself. But this time she smiled as she got back into her car and replied curtly, "Probably!"

She started the engine and pulled away thinking musically ... "*I'm gonna make a brand new start of it in old New York ...* ♪"

Lindy started packing, two blouses per day, jeans, dress pants, panties, and bras. Then she wondered to herself, "What if it gets cold?" She began adding sweaters, and heavy socks. Then she looked at the socks and giggled, thinking, "Cold in Pennsylvania—in July? I don't think so!" She removed the heavy clothing and then realized she had better go shopping just in case she'd missed something. She jumped into her car and made what she thought would be a quick visit to the mall. Two hours later she finally arrived back at her car, barely able to reach her keys as she juggled with arms full of clothing and incidentals.

When she arrived home, she proceeded to repack everything, carefully planning an outfit for each day as well as some dresses, in case they went out to one of the dances that Janey had described.

Finally, Theodore in hand, Lindy knocked on the door of her favorite neighbor Mrs. Miaorano. She was a petite, warm-hearted, Italian lady with an accent that was very thick, considering that she had been in America for almost fifty years. Mrs. Miaorano had been watching Theodore whenever Lindy had to go out of town on business. Lindy kissed her pet and told him to be good for Mama Miaorano.

Mama, as Lindy called her, could not say Theodore. In Mrs. Maiorano's words, the cat's name was "molto difficile (very difficult)," to say. Lindy put the cat down for a moment and Mama called to him, using her own name for the cat, "Mario vieni qui (Mario come here)."

With that, the cat ran to Mama and purred around her legs as Lindy threw her arms up and shouted, "My cat is bi-lingual and goes by the name Mario!" She turned and giggled to herself, "Sometimes life is just too funny."

She drove to the parking area of the airport and, as she pulled into the gate, the music from the radio played Sinatra crooning, *"I'm gonna make a brand new start of it in Old New York ♫."* The song echoed in her brain as she checked her bags. It stayed with her as she waited to board the plane, and as the aircraft taxied to the runway she tapped her fingers to the tune. Then, as the sleek jumbo jet took off, Lindy found herself singing softly to herself, *"It's up to you, New York ♪, New York ♪."*

Chapter Two

Jane Doe McMullen had a great sense of humor, which she probably developed over the years in no small part because of her name. It was her name, in fact, that brought her and Lindy Dennison together.

The girls didn't yet know one another, but shared the same homeroom in Newport Heights High School. On the first day of school, in the cafeteria, Chad, one of the football jocks, made a stupid and racist comment about her name, after hearing it called out in homeroom. "Maybe it's her slave name until they figure out who she belongs to." Jane was hurt by his comment, as she had never experienced prejudice growing up in California. Suddenly seemingly from out of nowhere, a beautiful, young strawberry blond girl walked over and proceeded to spill her coke all over Chad's Letterman's jacket.

She batted her eyelashes two or three times and said in her sweetest voice, "Gosh, I'm really sorry ... Chad."

Chad looked up into the face of an angel and said, "Gee, Lindy ..." But before he could finish his sentence, she continued, "I heard some idiot making a smart-alecky remark about my friend, and I came over to give him a piece of my mind. Did you see who it was, Chad?" She then batted her eyelashes a few more times causing Chad to get flustered.

"No ... no, Lindy, I sure didn't," he said sheepishly not wanting to admit his guilt. He then abruptly turned to the group and announced, "Nobody had better give Jane a hard time about her name, or they answer to me!"

The kids broke out in jeers and laughter as Lindy grabbed the seat nearest to Jane and said, "Hi, I'm Lindy Dennison." Jane extended her hand and quietly said,

"Thanks." The girls shook hands as Lindy continued, "Chad was in my class last year so I've got his number ... it's zero."

After that incident the girls became inseparable. Jane excelled in World and U.S. History, and was called upon by her best friend to tutor her well enough to pass her history exams. Although Lindy was strong in almost all her subjects, she couldn't see the importance of remembering all those obscure historical dates.

Instead, Lindy could be said to have *majored* in personality, and she became Jane's mentor in this "subject." The girls did almost everything together, and shared almost all their secrets, but Jane could sense that there was something wrong, something her best friend wouldn't talk about, for despite her great personality, Lindy had never kept a boyfriend around for very long. It seemed peculiar, and Jane could never get a straight answer about why Lindy would break up with them.

Those years together were the best years for both of them. But as adulthood approached, Lindy decided on college in Southern California and a major in business. Jane, on the other hand, felt compelled to pursue her higher education on the East Coast, majoring in U.S. History, which was to land her ultimately in a teaching career. Of course, this prevented the girls from seeing much of each other, but when they did, it felt to both as if no time had been lost.

Now, Jane stood in the JFK airport terminal impatiently, tapping her foot, waiting for Lindy's aircraft to arrive. Her jet-black hair fell in shoulder length curls, which she pulled back with a scrunchie because of the summer heat. Imitation Foster Grant's hid her green eyes, but was not enough to hide her beauty; as a teacher, she was every boy's dream. She, then, went over again to check the arrival board; Jane thought about how much she hated

16

waiting for planes. It gave her too much time to think, and that was hard to do at times.

She had married twice. Jane's first husband, Charlie Vickers, was a high school's version of Superfly, and as she used to comment, "His comb has the grease to prove it." She kept waiting for him to grow up, but it wasn't in his nature. So by the time her second year of college began, she and Mister Cool called it quits. For the next few years she doubted her judgment in guys, asking herself, "What were you thinking?" So instead, she focused on her education, keeping the boys at bay until she achieved her teaching credentials.

"God, where is the plane?" she thought as memories began to flood her consciousness. She tried to occupy her time by going through the airport magazine rack, but the recollections kept finding their way to the surface.

His name was Johnny McMullen, and he was her dream come true. Jane wasn't looking for the love of her life, but she was sure God had brought him to her. Johnny was six feet tall, with dark brown eyes and black hair. Johnny's heart was so big it could barely be contained in his chest, and people just gravitated toward him. He had come to New York from Denver, Colorado, because there was a desperate need for high school teachers in the boroughs, and he felt sure he could make a difference. He had been teaching at Jefferson High School for a few years, where he had developed a method to pique the interest of his kids. His lectures spoke of education as a transport from the inner city to endless possibilities and used examples of great men and women who did just that. Mr. McMullen listened in a way that made his students really feel he understood their problems.

As the new academic year started, Jane was sent to Jefferson High School for her first teaching assignment. Unable to find the room she had been assigned to, she had accidentally walked into Johnny's classroom. He stared at her, his mouth slightly open, until the laughter from his class made him aware of his obvious stupor. As she stood there unable to speak herself, Jane Doe Vickers fell madly in love.

Finally, when he found his voice again, Johnny said nervously, "May I help you?" There was a slight stutter as the words finally found their way out.

She stopped staring and introduced herself, "I'm Ms. Vickers. I'm the new history teacher." She felt strangely out of breath.

"You want room 201; it's the next room to the right."

She walked out the door of his room, and then quickly fell back against the wall of the building so as not to lose her balance. She took a deep breath. "Oh, my God!" was all that would come out.

That night she called her dear friend Lindy. "Lin … I'm in love, and I mean REAL LOVE." She went on to admit to her friend that they hadn't formally met yet. "But he's the one, Lindy … I just know it!" she exclaimed.

The next morning, in the teacher's lounge, the principal introduced them. Johnny wasted no time at all in getting to know her, and she him. They became an item on campus within a week, spending most of their evenings grading papers together, and learning about each other.

One night, midway through the second semester, he told Jane about a difference of opinion he had with one of the other teachers—something about one of the young kids he loved so much. As he told her about this incident, before he realized it, his voice began to grow louder and louder. Jane was finally able to break in momentarily: "Johnny, why are you yelling?"

He explained, "I come from a large, mixed family of Irish, Black, and a tiny bit of Italian, where yelling was always the normal way to communicate if you wanted to be heard." He warned her to try not to freak out if in his enthusiasm or anger, his voice began to bellow. "It's just my passionate emotional roots," he explained. She accepted this, saying, "I think I can get used to that."

Johnny was a considerate suitor and went out of his way to make Jane feel special and loved. He never missed an opportunity to surprise her, especially when she least expected it.

The night he proposed to her, he took her to an Italian restaurant. He had reserved a table, and on it was single red rose sitting in a crystal vase. The manager came over and mentioned, "He brought this over earlier today … isn't that romantic?" The waitress came over with two menus and two glasses of water. Johnny quickly seized his glass and took a large gulp. "Were you thirsty Hon?" Jane asked with a giggle. "I guess I was, babe," he said nervously, "now I have to go to the bathroom." Jane rolled her eyes with a smile.

After he left Jane began to notice how very crowded the large dining room had become. Suddenly she realized that both the manager and their waitress were still standing by the booth she was sharing with Johnny. People seated around the restaurant seemed to be looking at her and smiling. She was beginning to feel a little uncomfortable when unexpectedly from across the crowded dining room; a voice began singing ever so softly…

"And when I tell them how beautiful you are,
They'll never believe me…
They'll never believe me…
Your lips, your eyes, your cheeks, your hair are in a
class beyond compare.
You're the loveliest girl that one could see…

And when I tell them
And I'm certainly going to tell them
That you're the girl whose man someday I'll be.
They'll never believe me,
They'll never believe me,
That in this great big world you've chosen me."

By the time Johnny finished the song, he was on one knee in front of her. Then with tears in his eyes, he said, "Will you marry me?"

Everyone was cheering except Jane, who couldn't quite compose herself. Her mascara was running all down her face as she attempted to speak. The restaurant got very quiet as they waited for her response. Finally, she blurted out, "You bet I will!" The crowd applauded and yelled congratulations. Then Johnny wiped Jane's tears with a napkin and kissed her lips.

She found herself at the arrival board, 10-minute delay on the flight from Los Angeles. She muttered, "Shoot!" Her mind relentlessly wandered back to yesterday.

She and Johnny had talked about having children, but had decided to wait for a while so they could have some quality time with one another before starting the parenting years.

Johnny loved to make love with her, and she with him, and time had a way of standing still when they touched. Even his kisses burned their way through her flesh and into her soul. Afterwards he would caress her gently until she fell asleep. Often at this point he would move to the floor on her side of the bed, and just watch her for hours while she slept.

He told her once, "When you're asleep, all the stresses of the day are gone from your face, and I feel like a guard somehow able to keep the bad dreams from you—

and I really want to do that, babe." She loved it when he called her babe, and she loved being his wife.

Johnny was the kind of guy who couldn't turn his back on someone in need. While he was out buying Jane's annual single red rose in a crystal vase for their second anniversary, something caught his attention: He heard a woman scream in the mall parking lot. Johnny went running to see what was wrong, but he must have moved too quickly around the woman's car. A young and nervous thief with a small caliber handgun turned toward Johnny and pulled the trigger. Witnesses to the horrible crime said that as Johnny began to fall from the impact of the bullet, he dropped the crystal vase. As it fell, he grabbed the rose and called out, "Oh, my God ... No!" His other hand moved to his chest instinctively as his sweatshirt quickly changed to many shades of red. Paramedics tried unsuccessfully to save him, performing CPR on the way to the hospital, where a young emergency doctor pronounced him dead.

Jane went back to the arrival screen; it read another 10-minute delay. "They're never on time," she whispered, catching her breath, as the horrors of the bitter past threatened to overwhelm her.

She buried her soulmate three days after their anniversary. Jane had asked their friends not to send flowers but to give to a scholarship fund in his name instead. Johnny had always felt that education was the key to success. Near the casket was a single bright red rose in a crystal vase. After the church service, before the pallbearers took their position, a weeping Jane opened the casket one last time and placed the rose in Johnny's hand saying, "Goodbye, my love."

She could only remember bits and pieces of the next month. Lindy had come to help her best friend with the distressing job of going through Johnny's things and giving his clothes away. Lindy remembered when her grandfather died, how she and her mother sat and cried, as they smelled his clothes before packing them up for the Salvation Army. She knew that taking care of the little things at a time like this was very important. She had to keep reminding Jane that *moving on* is what her Johnny would want her to do. Most days and nights were spent talking and crying about Johnny, about how she loved and missed him.

Jane and Lindy were planning to go to the school to get his personal effects when there was a knock at the door. Opening it, the girls found themselves looking at the sad faces of Johnny's students, who were carrying a large box of his belongings. On the very top of his things was a leather-bound book with Jane's name on it. She opened the book and read:

My Darling Jane ...

I'm overwhelmed by you
To the point where words won't come
And so like a child discovering another marvel of the
world
I stand in awe of you
Until your eyes meet mine
And force me away ...

Honey—
These were my thoughts the first time I saw you.
J.

This book was filled with poems and short love notes, torn opera tickets and movie stubs, and pages of dates recording the main events of their life together. He had saved everything. Jane fingered the items tenderly. She turned a few more pages and another poem appeared.

Tears slowly fell from her cheeks as the words brought back precious memories:

The Kiss

As the dance began …
We moved to the rhythm of the saxophone
I could feel it coming …
The moment came closer
I knew you didn't want to feel for me …
You had promised yourself you wouldn't
But the music was so warm …
And I was persistent
I stared deep into your soul …
You began to quiver
My hand gently moved the hair that cascaded your face
My fingers touching skin so soft …
As they moved to the back of your neck
Your full lips attempted to say no …
But instead they only trembled
Awareness of the inevitable … became visible
Your beautiful green eyes finding mine …
The reflection of the candles shining through
I moved closer …
Waiting for resistance to be discarded for desire
Your warm breathe so close …
It moistened my lips
Finally a touch …
Soft and firm …
Tender and rough
As contact was made …
Then released …
Then made again
Lips parting slightly …
As our tongues brushed ever so lightly

The wetness of your mouth bathed me ...
As I became lost
For in my consciousness
There was only the kiss ...

Babe—
I can still feel you on my lips and it makes each day
better.
J.

Jane McMullen began to sob hard. She turned to Lindy and said, "I can't believe he did this." She finally came to the last page with a poem that he must have just finished. It was called "Happy Anniversary."

It's been quite a year...
Learning and unlearning
All we thought we knew
About the opposite sex and each other...
Quite a year...

With marvelous trips to Disneyland,
And arguments that border on grand.
Valentines and New York nights
And sometimes uncontrollable fights,
With words we wish we'd never said
Too late to bite our tongues instead.
But through the months the thing I find
Is you're always on my mind.
And one thing I have come to know
Is how much I really love you so...

Yes ... it's been quite a year
Quite a year indeed.

Sweetheart—
I know there have been some tough times, days
when you probably wondered what you had gotten
yourself into, for those days I'm so very sorry … For
all the others I wanted to say thank you with all my
heart.
J.

She closed the book and hugged it to her chest.

Jane looked up, "Thank God" she thought, "the plane is finally here." Thoughts of yesterday could now be placed carefully back into that special place deep inside her heart. Jane ran to the gate to meet her best friend in the world. She removed her sunglasses and wiped the tears from her eyes. Her biggest wish, she realized, was that Lindy might find that kind of love, even if only for a little while.

Heads turned as the shrieking sound of two beautiful and hysterical women greeting each other echoed through the terminal. Hugs and kisses, and mutual praise for appearance, resounded together in a lyrical hodgepodge of verbal resonance. The girls rushed through the airport to get Lindy's luggage. Male heads turned almost without thinking as beauty required recognition.

Jane pulled on her girlfriend's arm as she noticed a guy who, from behind, looked like the perfect ad for Levi jeans. As they stared at the form in front of them, the man turned around suddenly, feeling eyes on him, and as he did so he flashed a flirtatious smile at them. Shock came over Lindy and Jane, because the man was Brad Pitt, the movie star! Embarrassed at getting caught ogling an actor, they ran to the baggage section, still giggling all the way.

After retrieving Lindy's luggage, the girls settled in for the drive to Jane's home. Lindy did most of the talking, filling in for her best friend the details of the final encounter with Barry, and her feelings of relief at her choice. "I'm all right with my decision. Something inside of me said I needed to stop lying to myself about love—that it was time to let go of the dream and move on. So, dear friend, here I am."

Jane's home was a cute brownstone in the Long Island suburbs. Its solidity and antiquity hit her as Lindy entered the front door. Hardwood floors echoed slightly as she moved into the living room. The rugs that accented the room were woven in shades of forest green, giving the house a warm, welcoming feeling, and Lindy immediately felt at home.

There were two aged mahogany glass cases lined with black velvet against the dining room wall. Inside each were artifacts consisting of gold buttons, belt buckles, musket rounds, and delicate jewelry, all obviously from another time period. Pictures of Abe Lincoln and scenes of the Pennsylvanian countryside accented one of the alabaster white walls. Another wall held a collection of pictures of Jane's relatives and friends. In the middle of this collage were pictures of both Johnny and Lindy, which made Lindy feel very special.

She turned to Jane. "Boy, you've really gotten into this Civil War thing, haven't you?"

"Yeah, I guess so," replied Jane with a smile, "It started at an educational seminar when I met this teacher—Drake—and his wife who both taught at Penn State University. Their description of the Gettysburg reenactment held each year intrigued me—and you know how I am about history, especially Civil War history. I just couldn't resist their invitation to join them at the next Gettysburg reenactment." She continued getting more enthusiastic as she spoke, "When I arrived there, it was as if I had stepped back in time. Of course there were the typical reminders of the present, but I got such a sense of really being there in the past, and for a short time reliving it, that I was in heaven with the charade!"

She stopped when she noticed Lindy yawning, a sleepy expression on her face. "We'll have plenty of time to talk about it tomorrow, Lin. Let me help you put your bags away."

Once settled, the two sat for a while sipping wine and talking about old times, and the end of relationships. Jane hugged her friend tightly and said, "I love you so very much. I know I teased you about Barry, but I do understand what you're going through, and I want you to know I'm here for you."

Jane then reminded her friend they would be leaving early the next morning for Gettysburg, and that they should probably get some sleep. She kissed her friend's cheek and gave her a hug as they said goodnight.

Chapter Three

In the morning the girls were up early, excited and filled with anticipation about their adventure. They wasted no time loading the car and getting ready to go.

Lindy turned to Jane as the car sped down the interstate toward New Jersey, "Don't think for a minute I'm going to sit here and stare out the window all the way to Pennsylvania. I'll drive part of the way so you can rest too, Okay?"

"That's fine," Jane replied, "but for now sit back, listen, and enjoy the countryside." Jane embarked on a vivid and detailed picture of the past for her friend, switching to her *teacher* voice.

"Imagine a simpler time when roadways were made of rich, dark American soil, and all the vehicles were *one horsepower*. It was a time when the country was undergoing great change. Political philosophy had begun to polarize the North and the South, as economic differences became more pronounced. The South, with its rich soil, had become locked in a triangular trade pattern, with sugar, rum, and slaves as the currency. The plantations' need for more and more cheap labor had become necessary to run the ever-growing farms. At the same time, the North became more mechanized, creating industrialized cities in many places where farms used to be. A mass migration of people from rural farms and small townships to the newly developed cities was going on. It was as if our country was fast becoming two different worlds.

Oh, wow ... sorry," Jane interrupted herself. "I talk this way when I'm telling my students about the Civil War. I find it makes them get into it better than if I just give them dry facts and dates."

"That's just fine with me, Jane. I'm afraid my recollections, about U.S. history is not all that great, as you well remember. I love the way you're describing it; it makes it all come alive. Just pretend you're teaching your class, and I'll be your student, just like when you used to tutor me."

"Very well, but you asked for it." Jane then rearranged herself in the driver's seat, and then continued to weave her tale of the early American struggle to maintain its unity against opposing ideologies. Two hours went by. Lindy sat enthralled as she listened to Jane describe General Robert E. Lee's wrenching dilemma over his love of his state versus his loyalty to his country. Jane concluded by painting a vivid picture of the sacrifice of human lives and a war of horrific consequences.

"Perhaps now you can understand why this has become so important to me. I want my class to feel the pain of the women who lost their husbands, fathers, and brothers, so that they can appreciate that 'freedom for all' has a price, and those brave soldiers paid for it with their blood. The kids need to realize in their guts that freedom isn't free."

"Wow," was all that Lindy could muster up to say.

"So, are you ready to take over?" Jane asked. Receiving no immediate response from the history-stunned Lindy, she continued, "I need to go pee and stretch my legs soon." Noticing a sign for a service station up ahead, she said, "Eureka...there's a gas station and bladder relief."

Lindy just chuckled as Jane quickly moved across the expressway to the turn off and an opportunity to relieve herself. "From the way you're driving, I think I'd *better* take over," she said to her girlfriend as the car came to an abrupt stop. Jane ran inside; minutes later she came out with two cokes in her hand.

When Lindy took the wheel, with directions to take the 78 and then the 81 west to Harrisburg, Jane's conversation took a different turn.

"There's something else about Gettysburg, something I've been hesitant to mention up to now, Lindy."

"What's that?" Lindy asked, as she moved contentedly down the expressway.

"Well," said Jane, her eyes getting bigger as she spoke, "there are stories of strange things happening in and around the town of Gettysburg—things like ... ghosts!"

"Mmmm, like what kind of stories?" Lindy snickered then making a ghostly wail, "Ooouuh."

Jane's face, however, remained very serious as she began to relate a story she had heard while visiting the town where so many men had died:

> "Prentice Hall had worn many faces through the years, and it is said to have been some type of boarding school for young girls at just about the time of the Civil War. This story has been passed down year after year, and I've heard many versions of it. So I'll tell you the one that sounds the most accurate to me. One of the ravages of war is the displacing of families. During this unspeakable conflict, entire households were broken up, and children without parents would wander for food and shelter anywhere they could find them."

Jane, Lindy noted with pleasure, was now in full storytelling mode.

> "Such was the lot for the little boy who came upon Prentice Hall in the dead of winter 1862. The young women of the third floor of their schools dormitory happened upon the tiny fellow as he rummaged through the garbage outside their building. Taking

pity on him, they secreted him to their floor and put him in the room of Savannah Rose, a young girl with rebellion in her eyes and an inclination for trouble. Bringing someone into the rooms meant immediate expulsion; with the war raging just outside their window, bringing in any stranger was even more forbidden. The spinster who ran the school became suspicious, and decided to call an impromptu meeting of the young women, going door to door with instructions to meet without delay in the downstairs parlor. Fearful of getting caught with their small charge, Savannah and her friends instructed the boy to stand on the ledge outside the window, wrapped in a blanket, assuring him that as soon as the assembly was concluded, they would let him back inside. As his only alternative was to leave and weather the storm outside, a short time on the ledge did not seem too bad. The gathering in the sitting room was in its second hour before the girls were dismissed. They quickly ran to Savannah's room to retrieve the boy. However, when they threw open the window, there was no boy there to be retrieved. Only the blanket was lying outside the window on the narrow ledge. No footprints could be found on the narrow, snow-covered shelf. They concluded the worst, running back downstairs to the ground just under the third floor window, but upon their arrival at the spot where the child should surely have met his demise, they found nothing! No sign of footprints or clothing or blood were found in the only place he could have landed. The girls reentered the Hall, befuddled. They talked together about the little boy and what could have become of him, but no explanation could give them a sense of peace. Indeed, neither would the little boy find peace.

"It is said that on that very night, Savannah Rose woke to an uninvited guest tapping on her frosted glass window. When she saw a bluish young face staring through the window, she screamed in complete terror and ran from the room, hysterical.

"To this day, on cold, snowy winter nights, a face can often be seen hovering in the window of that third floor, looking in. It is the face of a small child bluish in color, freezing; with a wanting mournful look in his eyes. So often has this spectre appeared that he has been given the name "The Blue Boy." The latest sighting was only last year when a student was studying in that room on the third floor. The school has long since locked up all the windows and made them impossible to open, to avoid a lawsuit should anyone inadvertently fall out. The female student looked up from her textbook to see a hovering face, pinkish-blue, staring through the window at her. She looked down quickly and rubbed her eyes, and then looked up again to see the face moving to the left of the window, as if it were floating. That was enough for her! She ran downstairs quickly and told her schoolmates what she thought she had seen, adding that maybe she was just very tired and hadn't actually seen anything. She convinced a few of them to accompany her upstairs—if only for her own peace of mind, and to assure herself that fatigue had gotten the better of her. Upon entering the room, they looked toward the window, but saw no face moving around outside. As they all slowly approached closer to the frozen glass of the third floor window, though, they felt the color leave their faces as terror took hold—because, written on the window from outside, were the words EM PLEH!"

Jane looked over at Lindy and noticed her knuckles had whitened around the steering wheel. She reached over and pried her fingers loose. Lindy took a deep breath and made no comment. Jane wickedly loved this reaction, and decided to tell another eerie story, to see if she could turn her friend into a wreck before they arrived at their destination.

So, without warning, Jane began to speak again, but Lindy stopped her. "That scared me! Now *I* have to pee. I always have to go pee when I get frightened. I hope you're satisfied."

The car pulled into a gas station and out jumped the strawberry blond beauty. She disappeared for what seemed like just a moment and then reappeared and was behind the wheel again. Jane kept a straight face, but was cracking up inside at what she had accomplished, knowing full well that the next story should make her friend pee her pants for sure.

But instead Lindy requested a pause in the horror stories, reaching over to turn on the radio. After some knob adjusting and the standard static, an old Art Garfunkel tune began to play. He sang of *looking for the right one and when will the right one come along* ♩. As the song played, Lindy thought of her own search. Jane, always perceptive, noticed her companion becoming pensive and decided to give her some space to get through her feelings. But when the song ended, Jane began to relate her next tale.

"Remember the Penn State teacher I told you about, Professor Drake? Well, two of his colleagues were at a Gettysburg hotel attending a history symposium, which was scheduled to last a week. They, too, on their arrival, were told some interesting stories of areas around the town where people claimed to have had poltergeist encounters. They probably

33

snickered just like you did, until the third day of the conference. That day something happened that forever changed their minds about Gettysburg."

Lindy focused on the road, but despite her resolve, much of her attention became riveted on Jane's story.

"Having just left a very informative lecture on the Battle of Vicksburg, the two professors got into the elevator on the third floor of the hotel. There were four floors in the remodeled building, used by both the patrons and the hotel staff. There was also a basement, used to store supplies and retired furniture. The men pressed the first floor button, and as the doors of the elevator slowly creaked closed, they began discussing which local restaurant they should try this particular day. However, the doors did not open on the first floor as was expected. The men watched in amazement as the panel light moved instead to B, for basement." Jane paused, watching her friend's face as she continued her story, "Slowly the elevator doors opened to a scene that frightened the men beyond understanding. They found themselves in what appeared to be a makeshift operating room. There were sounds of men screaming, and a strong smell of blood. Artillery and gunfire could be heard outside the walls of the darkened room, the noise pounding through their brains. Their eyes bulged, staring in horror as doctors dressed in filthy gowns sawed off the arms and legs of conscious men hysterically screaming for death. Orderlies filled wheelbarrows full of discarded limbs and carted them to a nearby window, and then threw them out one by one. Suddenly the medical team stopped and looked over at the two men. As the screaming continued, two of the surgeons, perplexed at the sight of these unexpected visitors, began to move toward them. However, the elevator doors began to close as the ghoulish figures moved closer. When the elevator opened on the first floor, the two relieved college professors ran to the exit of the building, hearts pounding and minds never again absolutely sure what they believed about the topic of ghosts."

Jane felt the car swerve to the right as Lindy pulled off the side of the road and then ran into the bushes. A few minutes later Lindy peeked from around the brush and said, "You did that on purpose."

Jane couldn't hold her laughter anymore and started roaring as her girlfriend zipped up her jeans on her way back to the car.

Lindy spoke a bit sarcastically, though a small smile played around her lips. "Well, I should get a great nights sleep tonight, thank you very much, Jane. Thank you! Thank you! Thank you!"

Once finally through Harrisburg, after making the connection to the 15 south, it was a straight shot to Gettysburg. Jane talked a little about the quaint bed and breakfast she had stayed at for the past four years. "I've been hoping to run into a ghost or something. The place is said to have spirits floating around, but as of yet I haven't seen any. You'd think that after seeing me there year after year, they would make contact."

Lindy looked at her friend and smiled, "Let's change the subject for awhile so I don't have to keep stopping the car, all right?"

Jane agreed as the friends talked about the handsome soldiers that come from all over the country to be a part of the reenactment. As the car moved through the outskirts of Gettysburg, the girls began adjusting the dial of the radio until they captured Connie Francis singing *"Where*

---

the Boys are". They looked at each other and screamed in unison, then began to sing along with Connie at the top of their lungs. As the morning had started to make its way to early afternoon, both girls found themselves hoping the lyrics would come true.

Chapter Four

The car pulled slowly into the bed and breakfast called the Trostle House not far from Baltimore Pike. The girls jumped out, their excitement nearly palpable. The town was bustling with boys and men dressed in blue and gray uniforms and women and children clad in garments from an earlier time in American history. Both the girls felt a sensation of the time travel Jane had mentioned early into their trip. Staring at all the activity moving through the street, they got their luggage and headed to the front desk. Once registered, they were guided to the second floor. Jane was taken to Room 2 where she had stayed for the past four summers. Lindy was given room 5 just a few doors away. Lindy peeked into Jane's room as the innkeeper opened the door and placed her luggage inside by the dresser. The owners had gone to great lengths to give the room a period feeling using old black and white photographs and landscape paintings on wallpapered walls. The solid wood furniture increased the facade; the room contained early colonial chairs, and an oak dresser. There was even an antique cast iron bed with a beautiful patchwork bed spread.

Lindy remarked quietly, "Very charming," as she moved just slightly into Jane's room.

"I'm going to freshen up a little and do my nesting thing, and then I'll look in on you, okay?" Jane said, as she handed their host a few dollars and popped open her suitcase.

"Looks like I'm just a little down the hall. I'll do the same," replied Lindy, following the man with her bags.

Lindy slowly entered the room. Her eyes moved from one corner to the next, taking in the look and feel of 1863. It was very much like Jane's room. She also noticed that oddly, the room seemed to be growing colder with each passing moment. She turned, commenting to the innkeeper, "Great air conditioner." The robust jolly man said nothing, but smiled at her quizzically, raising one eyebrow. She handed him a tip and closed the door behind him. He left, pondering Lindy's comment, since the Inn had never had any air conditioning."

The room, just like Jane's description, breathed a simpler time. The chest of drawers was mahogany with brass handles that had been polished so many times the details had been worn smooth. She thought about all the things Jane had talked about in the car, and realized she was beginning to understand her friend's fascination with Gettysburg.

As she turned briefly back toward the door to get her bags, simultaneously she felt an extra cold, icy feeling move from her face to the back of her neck. Sensing a presence behind her in the room, she quickly turned around. Her eyes caught a fleeting shadow. Heart pounding, she looked out the window and sighed as she realized it had only been a plane overhead, momentarily blocking the sunlight from coming through her window.

My friend is too good a storyteller, she reassured herself with a nervous giggle. Still a bit shaken, Lindy began to hang her clothes and put her things in the proper drawers. She rearranged the furniture slightly and deposited her things in a way that made her feel more at home.

As she finished freshening up in the bathroom, Jane knocked on her door with a "Hey, neighbor."

Lindy called out, "Come on in."

"Very nice," commented her friend, as she inspected the room. "Lindy, are you almost ready? There's still plenty of the day left, and I thought we could get started."

Lindy decided not to mention her very strange experience. Instead, after inspecting her friend's attire she said, "Give me just a minute," pulling the shirt carefully over her head. "Let me just change my top."

Arm in arm, the girls strolled down the streets of Gettysburg, Jane acting as tour guide and describing all the wonderful gift shops and establishments that lent a strong ambience of a time gone by. Lindy felt overwhelmed by the ornate costumes adorning the many male and female re-enactors who came parading into view, commenting to Jane, "We'll have to dress up tomorrow." Lindy was like a little girl visiting Disneyland for the first time as her eyes were quite unable to take it all in.

Lindy's eyes were suddenly drawn to and then fixated on, one particular Union soldier standing off in the distance, apart from the others. She couldn't distinguish his rank from her vantage point, but she supposed he was some type of officer. She was intrigued by the way he looked at her; the handsome stranger was gazing at Lindy as though he recognized her—and she was enjoying the attention.

She turned to her sidekick. "Jane, do you see that soldier over there?"

Jane looked in the direction Lindy was pointing, and saw at least fifteen Union soldiers standing close together. "Cute, aren't they? But which one do you mean?" Lindy looked at her friend, bewildered. Why didn't Jane notice the soldier standing alone? But when Lindy looked again down the street where she had seen him, he was gone. She shrugged her shoulders as they turned and proceeded on their sightseeing tour of Gettysburg.

In and out of shops they traveled, down one avenue, then up another. While the two were engaged in the female ritual of shopping, an intrigued Lindy kept seeing her handsome soldier in the distance. On occasion he would move in her direction, and again she got the distinct impression that his attention was focused directly, and solely on her. She found herself wishing he would come up and say hello.

They ended the day's outing with a late dinner at the Farnsworth House Tavern, a local watering hole in the heart of the town. The bottle of Merlot that they shared complemented their steak dinner nicely. It also relaxed the two exhausted travelers enough that they were ready to call it a day.

But first Lindy turned to her comrade, kissed her cheek, and thanked her for her friendship and her wonderful suggestion to visit the past in this most unique way. She was beginning to appreciate Jane's connection to the town, and to the past it represented.

Jane kissed her back and said, "You have always been there for me in the worst of times, Lin, like a sister, and I love you." Both the girls felt tired so they strolled back to the Trostle House. Jane said, "I'll come by in the morning and we'll grab breakfast downstairs ... early, okay?"

Lindy nodded as she headed toward her room. Upon arriving there, she realized that all the adrenaline of the day had been used up. The sleepy young woman made her way to the bathroom, brushed her teeth, and gargled with the complementary mouthwash. She returned to the room and turned out the light. Unbuttoning the last button of her blouse, she made her way to the bed, letting the blouse drop to the floor. Then, looking down, she thought better of it, bent over and picked it up. "Perhaps," she thought, "that fine looking soldier will be around tomorrow. Maybe I'll say hello to him if he doesn't say it to me first." Thoughts of the day were swimming through her head when sleep finally overtook her.

Creaking sounds began to invade her slumber. The sound of someone or something moving back and forth across the floor brought her to consciousness, but she was too afraid to open her eyes. Fear, however, was taking its toll on her bladder, and she was forced to confront her intruder or explode. Lindy sat up in bed abruptly. No one was there, as she sat there freezing, afraid, and unable to speak. She heard the sound of the creaking floor moving quickly away from her. Then suddenly the door to her room began to shake violently, as if someone was shaking the door handle. Lindy jumped out of bed and ran to the toilet before her bladder floodgates opened up. Once back in bed, she stared at the door and stared some more until the sandman took her away again.

In the morning, after a shower and make-up detail, the girls met downstairs for breakfast. As Mrs. Sherman poured coffee, Lindy asked, "Is it your policy to check the doors to the rooms in the middle of the night?"

Mrs. Sherman, a hearty, red-cheeked woman, wiped her apron, looked blankly at her, and said, "Why no, dear."

Jane, however, had a question for Lindy after Mrs. Sherman left. "Why would you ask her that, Lindy?"

"Well," she responded, "last night I heard some strange creaking on the floor in my room, and when I sat up, the door started shaking violently. I just thought...quite frankly I don't know what I thought."

"Was it a ghost?" her old schoolmate inquired with mild indignation.

"I don't know!" Lindy said, and then continued sarcastically, "Perhaps it was a combination of a late dinner and an over-stimulated imagination brought on by the antics of an old friend!"

Jane began to laugh and announced to her blood sister, "I did go a little overboard yesterday, but the truth of the matter is that this place has, in fact, been known to have visitors from the past. Right, Mr. Sherman?"

Mr. Sherman, the innkeeper, was approaching their table. He always swore he was descended from General William T. Sherman of the Union Army. He nodded in agreement as he came up to their table and then went on to say, "We've had our share of spirit visits, but I don't recall

anything ever being seen or heard in that particular room."
He told the attentive ladies, "Mary and I bought the Inn only
seven years ago. Before that, a Mr. Trostle owned it. The
place had been in his family since the time of the great
conflict. It was even used as a sort of hospital for the Union
forces."

Jane announced, "Okay, then … no ghost. That
makes me feel a little better, considering I've been coming
here for four years, and by this time any spirits running
around these halls should know me on sight."

Lindy remarked that maybe Jane was slightly
jealous at the possibility her comrade might have been
visited by the spirit world.

Jane, ashamed of herself, admitted, "I'm sorry.
You're right—I've been hoping to get visited by a ghost for
years now, and…nothing, always nothing"

Lindy, feeling sorry for Jane, made a promise to her
friend, "Then if I see another … something I'll call you.
Agreed?" She confirmed the verbal pact with a handshake.

As they finished their breakfast, Mr. Sherman talked
at length about how his famous ancestor had laid siege to
the city of Atlanta and burned it literally to the ground. He
rambled on in detail, the destruction of the railroad lines,
and how Sherman melted down the rails and had them
twisted around the trees. "This act of war became known
as Sherman's neck ties," the innkeeper said proudly.
"When the general was questioned about his destructive
acts, he responded that 'war is cruelty.' That's something
you'll come to know if you listen to the stories of the park
rangers. You know …"

At this point the girls looked at each other, raised
their eyebrows, and commented in unison, "Well, we had
better get started with our day."

Mrs. Sherman, realizing her husband had once more
gotten carried away, elbowed him fondly in the stomach

and then turned to the girls, "You young people get going and don't pay him any mind."

Although Jane had previously purchased authentic clothing for herself, she felt compelled to shop with Lindy fearing a sale might be in progress, and she would miss it. They went from one shop to another picking out skirts, pantaloons, corsets, slips of the day, blouses, hats, and all the other artifacts that made a woman look proper in the 1860s. Finally, at a curio shop, Lindy found a beautiful cameo on a black alabaster background trimmed in gold.

She paid the cashier, and then turned to get Jane's attention from across the store. After she turned around, Lindy suddenly found herself looking up into the face of the handsome soldier from the day before. She felt ice-cold air moving across her face. Startled, she dropped the bags containing the day's procurements. She bent over to pick up her things, but when she looked up the soldier was nowhere to be found.

She immediately called out to Jane, who was standing near the store's entrance, "It was him, again! Did you see where he went?"

Jane looked over at her, perplexed. "Where did *who* go? No handsome soldier passed me, darling; I think I would have noticed," exclaimed Jane with a smile. Her smile, however, disappeared when she noticed that Lindy had grown very pale. "Lin, I think your blood sugar is low. We've been going at it since breakfast, and it's almost five o'clock. Let's go around the corner to the Dobbin House Tavern. I've been there before, and the food is great. We can grab a bite before you collapse."

Lindy agreed, and the two went arm in arm to the pub. While they were waiting for their food to arrive, Lindy reached into her purse and pulled out a pen. She opened her paper napkin and began to draw a soldier's uniform. As she drew something on each shoulder, she asked Jane, "What are these thingies and what do they signify?"

"Those are captain's bars. Why?" Jane asked her friend.

"That's what my soldier was wearing. God...he was so gorgeous. I can't believe that you, of all people, didn't see a guy like him! I was sure he was going to talk to me; I could see it in his beautiful blue-green eyes." Lindy breathed a heavy sigh, and then decided to drop the subject.

They spent the rest of the evening listening to the locals tell tales of spirits wandering through Gettysburg, and recalling the battle areas where so many lost their lives.

The moon, nearing full, found its way to the highest point in the sky when the girls said goodnight to one another. Lindy felt she needed to try on her new clothes before she would be able to retire peacefully. As she was removing her clothing, she felt a chill begin, and her nipples responded to the change immediately. She warmed them with her palms and then quickly began to dress. Once all the new garments were in place to create a complete outfit, she went to the dresser mirror and pulled up her hair with a clip. Looking at her reflection, she fastened the cameo over the top button of her new blouse. She smiled to herself at how authentic she looked. The icy cold again found its way through her as she stood by the mirror. She moved out to the small balcony and looked up at the wondrous moon in its semi-entire splendor. She stood there thinking of how lonely she was, and how her life was changing again. Then she slowly walked back inside and removed her new things, placing them neatly on the chair. The air conditioner seemed to cool some spots in the room more than others, and also moved around oddly, sometimes chilling her to the bone. But since it had been terribly warm and humid all day, the cold felt very welcome. She got into bed and settled in for a relaxing, tranquil night's sleep.

Chapter Five

The incredible sadness of the Captain had gone on for so many years he had stopped caring about anything at all. Time seemed to be marked by the change of music that moved through the walls of his self-imposed prison. From the time of his death, he had remained on the second floor of the Trostle House. He had no desire to go outside, no desire to move, or talk—or even care. Daniel's extreme depression left him with no desire to feel. The trauma to his heart that came with losing both his love and his life had trapped him in a space between earth and eternal rest, and he had lost the will to move to the next plane on his immortal soul's journey to heaven.

As the sun made its way through the window of the room where he had taken his last corporeal breath, Captain Daniel Sutherland did what he always did. He searched his soul and scoured his mind, desperately reliving his last days in an attempt to find some reason, some justification, for what had transpired…

* * *

Daniel recalled the battlefields scattered with the bodies of young men he had grown to love, the mortally wounded, were quickly replaced with fresh troops after each Confederate encounter. So it was that each night he wrote to the family members of those that had fallen, at the same time mailing a list of all the deceased to the postmaster. In this way he could ensure that all their parents, siblings, and wives could be notified. This was no easy task for him. He knew that there would be no way to comfort them or to put down in words how important their sacrifice was to the country they had loved.

His mind drifted to his beloved. Daniel thought, how patient Sarah was through their separation. Neither one of them thought the war would wage on for more than a few months, but now after over 3 months apart, he wondered if he would ever see her again. She had expressed her love to him in such a lovely fashion, her words etched into his memory. *"I am yours my love, without reservation. You and I are two halves of one soul. I will wait for you no matter how long you are gone."* Sarah wrote in one of her last letters to him, but he hadn't heard from her since that correspondence.

Sporadically, small numbers of young men were being assigned to him from his home state of Connecticut and other cities from the North. News of home came usually from those that were sent to reinforce the front, as the mail was almost two to three months behind. Daniel had not received a letter from Sarah Elizabeth McKee in at least that long, and he was starved for word from his "one true love." He wrote her religiously every day, mostly of his plans for them to start their life together, a life that had been placed on hold by the needs of the nation he also loved.

So when the few new recruits arrived at the 27th Connecticut camp, hungry eyes and ears surrounded them as the news from home was verbally distributed to the homesick men. Three of the young replacements, from Daniel's hometown of Huntington, stared at him in the most peculiar way. Jed Montgomery, who had been like a younger brother to Daniel, ran to the Captain and almost threw his arms around him, but stopped short remembering his rank.

"Private Jedidiah Montgomery reporting for duty, sir," he said, staring at his superior.

"Welcome to hell, soldiers," the Captain announced to the new men. Then Daniel leaned over and whispered into Jed's ear, "Good to see you, lad." The new men's continued stares finally brought forth the question. "Why are you boys looking at me so strangely?" Daniel asked his homeland replacements.

"We received word that you lost your life long about three months ago," Private Edward Biddle blurted out.

"We thought you were dead, sir," Jed said and then continued in the same breath "It is so good to see you alive, Captain."

Daniel stood for a moment in silence, trying to take in the information he had just received. His expression turned grim. He thought then of Sarah and why he had not received a letter. His mind began to race through the implications of what the young men had just said, as he realized that this erroneous information had made its way to his love. He thought of her pain and what he could do about it. "My God, I must get word to her that I'm alive," he thought desperately to himself. He shook his head. "Wouldn't my letters have assured her that this news was false?"

Jed could see the panic that had quickly overtaken his commander's face. He became worried about what he had to reveal next to the man who had been his role model while he was growing up.

The Captain grabbed Jed's shoulders in his powerful, desperate hands, and in a voice wrought with emotion asked, "What of Sarah? Does she think I'm dead?" His mind was reeling over what he imagined she must have been going through.

Jed did not answer right away. He looked away from his hero's frantic eyes.

"Jed?" The Captain demanded, "Is she all right?"

Jed, aware that his silence may have given Daniel the idea that she might have taken her own life from the tragic news quickly responded, "She's okay, Captain...but she's ..." Jed was having a very hard time getting it out.

Daniel squeezed Jed's shoulders harder. Jed cried out abruptly "She's married, sir!"

The powerful hands continued to apply pressure to Jed's arms out of reflex, and the Captain's eyes became a reservoir as he stared at the bearer of the news.

"Captain!" screamed Jed, as the pain to his shoulders became unbearable.

Daniel dropped his arms and his head. Then he turned toward the sunset and looked up, silent tears held back by his duty to maintain his dignity in front of the men who had come to depend on his strength. "How many sunsets had he shared with her?" he thought. "What was it she had said?"

"My love for you is like the colors of the sun setting in the West, so warm and beautiful that it will sustain you through the darkest night."

"Sarah ... oh my Sarah ... now there is nothing to sustain me." The Captain limped slowly into his tent, closed the canvas entrance, and sat alone with an army blanket pressed firmly to his face, attempting to muffle the sound of his broken heart, as all his emotion had to be released. He tried hard not to be heard by the troops, who stood outside and had become aware of his anguish.

The encampment became solemnly quiet as the men stood watch over their leader's shelter. Eyes watered at hearing their brave captain's suffering. The quite darkness interrupted occasionally by the sound of a hoot owl whose voice echoed his haunting questioning through the night.

After hours of nightfall, Jed Montgomery sat in his new temporary home, preparing a letter to his mother. He wrote of the many young faces just like his own, all dreaming of Mom's homemade chocolate cake. He heard them trying to say simple prayers to a God they didn't know, and he wondered as he wrote how many would die in the days ahead. He was frightened, but proud to be among them. As he sealed his letter, one by one those lads who didn't know how to write approached him with requests to write to the ones they loved. Jed had always wanted to be a writer, but he never expected his career to begin in a tent outside the town of Gettysburg.

The following morning Jed had been ordered to the Captain's quarters. Once inside and alone, Jed ran into his hero's arms. Daniel embraced the lad, who used to follow him around every time he came to Huntington for farming supplies. Daniel had so many questions that he was not sure where to begin. However, as Jed relayed in more detail the events leading up to his departure from home, the officer began to understand. Jed described how Sarah had been destroyed by the news and how Thomas had been there to console her.

It appeared that Daniel's oldest and best friend, Thomas Paine, named after the famous Revolutionary War leader, had married his Sarah. As the Postmaster of Huntington, it was Thomas' responsibility to inform the next of kin whenever word came from the war. Jed said that, upon seeing his best friend's name on the list, Thomas, being close to both Daniel and Sarah, had helped Sarah deal with the devastating news. Thomas had thus taken it upon himself to see her through an almost impossible time.

Daniel thought perhaps marrying Sarah was Thomas' way of repaying him for saving his life so many years before, when they were still very young. Daniel had been hunting in the forest near Charter Oak by the Housatonic River outside Huntington when he came upon his friend lying in the brush. Tom's horse had taken a fall and crushed Tom's left leg. Not having a horse of his own, Daniel picked up his friend and carried him over five miles to the doctor's office. They were able to save his leg, but enough damage had been done to leave the boy with a permanent limp. This injury also kept Thomas from joining his friend on the battlefield.

According to Jedidiah, after just two months of spending so much time together, Thomas and Sarah were wed. Bewildered, Daniel wondered to himself, "How could she go on with her life so easily. Had I spent so much time in my military career that somehow my importance to her could have been misconstrued as anything less than it was? What of all my letters written over the last three months? Had the mail been so slow as not to reach her in time to know the announcement of my death was in error? Or did my letters get lost somehow?" Daniel's head was hurting; he couldn't handle knowing any more details at the moment. He dismissed the private. Jed saluted his hero and left the tent.

Meanwhile Daniel's heart was in unfathomable pain. It wouldn't go away no matter how hard he tried not to think about it.

The next morning, the Captain's brows furrowed with worry as he received reports of a major Confederate build up on the outskirts of Gettysburg. His men saw the change in their leader and feared what might lie ahead for them. Doctor Muny was seen coming from the Captain's tent, swearing and ranting. "If you're not going to take care of that damn leg, I'll cut the damn thing off."

As he recalled that final conflict, Captain Daniel Sutherland had known all too well that his forces were outnumbered. But, being a scholar in the art of war, he knew that if his strategy was successful, many of his men's lives might be saved. He had met with his commanding officer Colonel Edward E. Cross to get approval for his battle proposal. Colonel Cross was a tall, imposing figure of a man. He himself was only 31 years old, prematurely balding with a reddish beard and a reputation for being cool and brave under fire. He liked Daniel's strategy and decided to join them on the battlefield. Daniel returned to his unit and related the first part of the scheme to his lieutenants, who voiced their agreement and went out to prepare the troops. The second component would require the assistance of only one person, and this part he kept even from his commander.

The Captain ordered Jed Montgomery to his tent the morning of the operation and proceeded to explain to him the details of his plan and what he required from young Jed.

"It's insane!" replied the young soldier who quickly followed his statement with, "sir."

Daniel then educated his young private, "When the Spanish were fighting the Moors, they too were outnumbered, and their leader was wounded badly. Without their commander to lead them, they would lose hope and surely be defeated. So the officer had himself strapped into his saddle so that even if he died with his armor on, he would appear to be all right, giving his men the desire and the will to fight on."

"Did it work, sir?" asked Jed.

"Yes, Jed, although their commander was killed while strapped in the saddle, his position on the battlefield not only gave his men courage, but his unwavering presence in the saddle frightened the Moors so severely that they retreated back to their own country."

He looked deep into the eyes of the boy he loved like a little brother and continued, "These men outside have become my family. I can look at them and see the fear and uncertainty of what is to come. They need to know that I will do my best to get them through this horror. Besides, Jed with this leg of mine the way it is, I'll never get up if I fall off my horse. They need to see me upright on the battlefield." That's where you come in, Jed." With that the

Captain patted his friend's face gently and said, "Let's get going, son."

Once outside the tent, Jed then securely fastened his hero into the saddle and saluted as the Captain rode out to take command of his troops.

"Move out, men!" said the Captain, as the men positioned themselves behind him, ready to engage their brothers in gray.

Daniel looked to his right as Colonel Cross suddenly rode up beside him and said, "Let's charge 'em like hell, Captain."

Certain that the enemy would expect a forward advance, Captain Sutherland began to lead a company of his men right up the middle of the wheat field, maintaining their distance from the onslaught of confederate artillery that exploded just in front of their position. His rag-tag group of weathered warriors looked as if they had seen too many battles, while their Confederate counterparts moved decisively to engage and annihilate them. The Gray officers assumed that their intelligence reports had overestimated the Union numbers as they viewed the pitiful display advancing toward them.

Then, just before frontal contact was to be made, the 27th Connecticut Sharpshooters who flanked both sides of the grain crop, hidden beneath the tall grass, began to pick off the Confederate soldiers, taking up the rear of the advancing troops with long-distance accuracy. This maneuver afforded the Captain and his men protection, as fifty of his men from each side of the wheat field caused chaos for the rebel troops—now unsure in what direction to go, and whether to fight or flee.

Just before the Colonel could give the order to charge, he was shot in the stomach and fell off his steed.

The Captain watched as his commander went down and instinctively screamed, "Charge!" Then he rode his chestnut stallion gallantly toward the Confederate ranks, his sword slicing through all who posed a danger to his men. A 69-caliber musket round struck Daniel's right arm as his military saber was raised, the metal ball shattering the humerus bone as it traversed through his limb. With total disregard for the obvious pain, Daniel transferred the sword to his left hand and continued battling onward. His bravery inspired his men as he struggled through the rebel ranks.

Then Daniel was struck again. A lead mini-ball ripped ferociously through his right chest exiting out his back, taking his flesh along with it. But it appeared nothing could stop the harnessed officer as he rode through the Gettysburg wheat field under continued fire.

Upon seeing the courageous Union soldier still upright in his saddle after being shot in repeated attempts to bring him down, the enemy became fearful that this phantom on horseback could not die. As the superstitious rebels fell back in retreat, they made every effort to kill the specter with the waving saber. The Union soldiers cried out as their gallant leader was struck again and again by the destructive force of the soft lead balls. They fought savagely to halt the Southern attack on their hero and finally succeeded in forcing the ultimate withdrawal of the Gray military.

The men of the 27th Connecticut regiment moved toward their brave Captain, still upright in his saddle.

He looked down on them, "Nice work, men." With that he lost consciousness, and the men who loved him carried him to the nearby Trostle House, which had been converted into a field hospital of sorts for the Union wounded. Doctor Jim Muny directed the men to carry the Captain upstairs to a private room and then proceeded to examine the young officer. After removing Daniel's uniform, the doctor looked in horror at the devastation of the battle manifest on the Captain's body. The men standing in the doorway were unable to hold back their tears as they stared at the multiple wounds. The look on the medical man's face said clearly that the end of their hero was near.

Doctor Muny made every effort to make him comfortable as the barely conscious Captain moved his eyes slowly toward the door of the room, whispering, "Gentlemen, it has been my greatest honor to serve with you." With that his eyes began to become lost in an eternal upward gaze. His lips moved one last time, and a muffled sound arose from deep within his chest. "SARAH," he cried, and as the name crossed his lips, death finally found him.

Suddenly Daniel Sutherland found himself looking down at the war-torn body that had housed him. He watched for the longest time as his body was wrapped in clean white linen and his men came in one by one to pay their respects to their beloved Captain. Then things got very very dark and it remained that way for some time.

Unexpectedly and without warning, Daniel began to see his life flash across his mind's eye. Then he began to see a brilliant light through his tunnel-like vision. As it got brighter, Daniel's memory kept returning to the moment he was told about his Sarah being wed. It was as if the light were calling him to go, but the face of Jed Montgomery and his lips proclaiming those impossible words prevented his advancement.

The light had begun to decrease in size, until it finally disappeared. Daniel looked around and found himself back in the room of the Trostle House. It was dark and he was alone. He began to sob openly, unable to contain himself. All the pain of his losing Sarah became an uncontrollable, horrible echoing wail into the void of his unknown existence.

*　　*　　*

Time for Daniel moved just as it did for the living, but he didn't concern himself with the world he viewed from his chamber. He watched quietly from the upper corner of the room as the door opened and strangers walked in unpacked stayed a day or two, and left again. Year after year he remained uninterested in this ritual of strangers invading his solitude, for the Captain had fallen into a terrible state of depression. He resided in the corner of the ceiling; unnoticed by the strangers or by time. Occasionally, a couple would make love under his watchful eye, but it only reminded him of his last night with Sarah.

Music from a thing called a radio showed up one year, and the Captain was amazed at how its sound filled the room. However, as the years moved forward, the music became louder and the lyrics incomprehensible. He began to cringe each time the music box was turned on.

So it was for Daniel. Now close to 136 years had gone by, and the pain in his heart made it seem as if it had been only a moment since the words about Sarah's marriage had crossed Jed Montgomery's lips.

On this particular day, after his customary review of his life on earth, the door handle began to move, just as it had done countless times before. Then it moved again. Daniel felt an urgent, unfamiliar need to look. Suddenly, when the door opened, behind the overstuffed innkeeper stood the woman he loved … his Sarah. Daniel's eyes filled with love as he moved down slowly from the ceiling of the room toward her. His heart began to beat again, and he felt himself smile as tears ran freely down his face. He stared at her in disbelief. Slowly he moved to touch her, his hands shaking in anticipation. Sarah had gotten a bit older, and had cut her hair, but it was she. "How," he thought to himself, "could this be possible?"

The Captain tried to embrace her as she simultaneously spoke: "Great air conditioner." But found that his arms moved through her. He became overwhelmed by powerful feelings. Very quickly, he moved back into the corner, after being bombarded with the sadness that emanated from her. Somehow Daniel was able to learn about her as his hands passed through her. "You are not my Sarah!" he addressed her in thought. Daniel stared, confused and dazed by her resemblance to his beloved, and he was astonished at his ability to absorb into his being the emotion, memories, and thoughts that lay under her smile.

The young woman began to put things away, and he found himself moving closer again to find out more, as her memories became his. Images of her father walking out of her life when she was but a child came to him first. As she moved about the room nesting and making the room homier, he felt like he was dancing with her and around her, taking in more of her past. She was waltzing unknowingly through the chamber with a curious spirit. She had learned to hide her pain behind beautiful eyes he had begun to understand. So despite the fact that she was not his Sarah, he found himself hopelessly drawn to her.

Another image came to him from her subconscious mind: a cousin, Christina, who was more like a sister during this Sarah look-a-like's youth, had gotten severely ill and died suddenly before the young woman could tell her how much she loved her or even say goodbye. For that, she was angry with God. Daniel must know more. He made another pass. There were walls and barriers, memories so painful for her that she hid them from herself. Their shared pain ended the dance abruptly. Daniel fell back exhausted by the strange encounter.

This was a strange, new, frightening experience for him, and he found himself unable to move—as if he were in some way paralyzed in place. He looked across the room while the lady moved about the bathroom. Out of the blue, the Captain heard a knock at the door, and the beautiful Sarah-woman passed through him on her way to answer it.

Another beautiful female entered and called the Sarah-woman *Lindy*. "Lindy," he thought to himself. Just as this thought was passing through Daniel's mind, Lindy began removing her blouse and walked through him again, saying, "Let me just change my top." With that the two were gone from the room, leaving Daniel immobilized by the ordeal.

He stood there motionless for some time, unsure of what might lie beyond the doors that had imprisoned and protected him for so long from the unknown. He wondered to himself, "How long have I only imagined that face I love? Do I dare lose another moment to the depression within my heart? What cruel joke has the Almighty decided to play on a soul already as lost as I have become?" The temptation to understand more was greater than he could resist. So, with immense apprehension, he slowly moved through the bedroom wall of the Trostle House, past his memory of bloody battlefields and torturous death, and out the door into the mysterious world outside.

As the Captain moved onto the strange-looking, blackened roadway, he looked down and proceeded to pound his boots on the blacktop. He then slowly raised his head toward the summer sun, but found he was unable to feel its warmth on his face, which was a special feeling he could only remember now. Daniel then turned abruptly as a fast-moving carriage without a horse passed through his transparent body. "What manner of transportation might that be?" he thought to himself, shaking his head in amazement.

Buildings he clearly remembered looked polished and new. The terrible battlefields all around the make-shift hospital had become fields of beautiful green grass and seemed to be lined with statues of some sort in different shapes and sizes as far as the eye could see. As he walked from one memorial to another, the Captain realized that too many boys had died here. Questions that had been buried inside him started to make their way to his consciousness, and they were being answered as he viewed the horizon. An American flag waved high atop a flagpole adjacent to a large building. "The Union has survived...thank God," was his first thought, "But there are so many more stars!" came next. He attempted to count them, but the wind made it difficult. Still he persisted. "Fifty stars for fifty states—my God!" he exclaimed.

Daniel walked for hours as he reviewed each memorial and the lists of the fallen heroes that had been placed upon them. It was early afternoon when he finally found his company's name engraved on a granite stone. He went down the list as his crystal blue-green eyes focused on each name. All those names had faces and all the faces were family to him. Then, apart from the list of names, he found his own name larger than the rest, with the simple words underneath it, *Beloved Captain*. He slowly turned away and then remembered about young Jed. He turned back and reviewed the list again, but there was no mention of Jed Montgomery. Had he somehow survived the trauma that was Gettysburg? He prayed to God that this was true, for he loved the young boy greatly.

Thoughts of his Sarah flashed back into his mind, and so he made his way toward town to find the Lindy person. Halfway down the main street, he saw her again... "Lindy," he reminded himself again as his lips almost uttered, "Sarah." He watched as she got her friend's attention and pointed at him. He quickly looked to his rear assuming that she must be looking at something behind him, but, no, there she was in the distance looking right at him. Her girlfriend made a comment and grabbed Lindy, directing her to a clothing shop of sorts. The Captain kept his distance as he followed the two women from one place to another. He found himself moving only slightly closer, and on occasion his eyes made contact with Lindy's.

Finally, late into the evening, he watched from the street as the two friends entered his sanctuary.

"There is so much I would like to know about her," he thought longingly as he made his way back to his room. It was very late, and as he entered his room, he found Lindy asleep in the bed. He moved very close to her and then walked to the other side of the room. Back and forth he paced across the room, unsure of what to do. Suddenly, she sat up in bed, startling the Captain. Afraid she would see him and be frightened, he ran frantically through the door of the room, the doorway rattling as he moved through it.

The Captain strolled through the night revisiting the violent wheat field and Devil's Den. As he rested on a giant stone that overlooked a beautiful forest, the gentleman from Connecticut tried hard to understand what was happening to him.

Suddenly he heard a voice in the distance, calling out, "Bluecoat." Daniel turned to see a bearded lad in a tattered gray uniform standing on a nearby boulder. The young man approached the Captain; his hand stretched out, and said, "I haven't seen you before, Captain." Their hands met, and the Captain noticed that he could feel the strong grip of the young man.

A bit suspicious, he answered, "I've been around."

The young Confederate soldier smiled and then laughed loudly as he announced, "Don't worry, Captain. The war's been over for almost 140 years."

"Really?" the officer responded in surprise.

"Name's Timothy," the soldier said. "You sure don't act like any ghost I've run into."

The Captain admitted to his one-time enemy that he had remained in the room where he had died on July the second, 1863.

"That's a long time to be in one place ... I died here at Devil's Den. It was sure a terrible fight and we was

winning when I was plugged by one of your sharpshooters."
The soldier placed a finger into the hole in his shirt.

Daniel started to ask about their shared condition
and the parameters of their existence, but he was quickly
interrupted.

"Sorry, Cap'n, I can't help you with that ... even we
have rules." Timothy chuckled and began to float away.
"See ya, Cap'n."

Daniel yelled, "Wait!" but young Timothy had already
disappeared. Captain Sutherland sat down on the boulder
at Devil's Den and began to analyze his situation, going
over the past few hours. He concluded that when he was
on the street, hoping strongly that Lindy would see him, it
seemed that she did. But when he walked back and forth in
his room tonight, not wanting his presence to be known—
although he was sure that she somehow vaguely sensed
his presence even then—Lindy, in fact, could not see him.
Perhaps, then, he had some control in this regard.

An experiment was needed. The Captain jumped off
the mossy rock and headed towards the woods, his
concentration intent on not being seen by anyone. He
came upon a deer drinking from the creek. Daniel was sure
by the animal's behavior that it knew something was amiss,
he moved closer until he was face to face with it. However,
the animal didn't move; it just remained motionless as it
stared in his direction. Once sure that this was not a
coincidence, he thought himself visible, and in that instant
the deer jumped away and was lost from sight within
seconds. The limitations of his existence were beginning to
become clearer, but his purpose had not yet become
known. He was sure, however, that it involved the beautiful
Lindy Dennison.

Chapter Six

Daniel Sutherland watched the beautiful Pennsylvanian sunrise, and although his senses had undergone a kind of metamorphosis, his memory was intact. He could recall the coolness of the morning and the beginning warmth from the sun as it began its journey across the sky. The rainbow of colors that decorated this planet moved across his view and he was in awe. The breathtaking splendor of the world before him, made Daniel wonder about God's eternal plan and how he fit into it. He pondered the glory of love—the joy and happiness it could bring, and the unending horror of its loss.

He decided to take some time to acquaint himself with the new world he was seeing around him. People drove by in the horseless carriages. Families walked by him, and many carried cameras so small that they fit around their necks. There was so much that had changed, and yet, oddly, all around him were soldiers and people dressed just like him. He was a bit confused, and Timothy hadn't been much help. The Captain had become lost in his thoughts; morning had ended, and the afternoon was beginning to pass by.

Daniel found himself walking in circles as he tried to take in all the new and unusual sites on his way into the small town and the world of tomorrow. There were people in short pants and women with almost nothing on at all. He felt embarrassed, and he quickly looked away. The whole town had a festive look about it. He looked up at a banner that commemorated the Battle of Gettysburg and announced the 135th annual reenactment. Daniel did the math and began to understand just how much time had passed, which explained all the incredible things he was seeing.

Unexpectedly, he caught a glimpse of the two girls making their way into a quaint little curio shop. He felt compelled to make his appearance known again to Lindy, but was still a bit unsure about how to do it, except by somehow willing it. He entered the mercantile unseen and moved toward Lindy. She had just purchased an item as he came up behind her. She turned quickly then, and he found himself staring into the most beautiful eyes he had seen in over a hundred and thirty-six years. And Lindy was staring back, totally lost in his gaze. Flustered, she dropped all her packages, and in that instant he was gone.

The Captain was confused and apprehensive his emotions still unable to separate Sarah from Lindy. He wanted to hug her and never let her go, or shake her, demanding answers to his eternal questions. He needed time to think and decide what to do. So as Lindy called to her friend Jane to find the tall, handsome officer, the Captain was making his way to the only place he could find solace. There he remained for many hours, alone, until he heard the key slide into the lock and the door to his solitude open again.

She moved through the door with some difficulty, her arms full of packages. She placed them on the bed and began to arrange her newfound treasures. The Captain stared as Lindy began to remove her clothes. He was astonished at how much the process was like a dance. Slowly, she removed one article after another, letting them drop to the floor. The Captain found himself moving with her, remembering that last night with Sarah. Once she was completely naked, the cold air that moved around her caused her to warm her erect nipples with her hands. Then she began to pick up the antique undergarments and put each on in turn. One piece of clothing after another she danced, until at last she stood before the oval antique mirror in the corner of the room. The cameo broach over the top button of her blouse was centered perfectly. Then she pulled up her hair and pinned it back.

The Captain stared as he saw his soulmate's reflection in the mirror, and unable to contain himself, he let out a sigh, as he adored her incredible beauty. Startled, she turned abruptly and, seeing nothing, thought, "It must be the wind." She turned back to her reflection, happy with the final result. The Captain continued to move near her. She went to the balcony, stood there enjoying the warm night air, and looked out at the moonlit evening. She thought about how it would be to find someone to love completely. She even began to entertain the thought of her elusive stranger as a candidate. Lindy giggled to herself as she returned inside and picked up her discarded clothes. Then she delicately removed the new garments and placed them neatly folded on the chair by her bed, preparing to retire for the evening.

As dreams made their way into her unconscious, the handsome officer appeared before her. He stared at her for quite some time before he spoke: "Madam, I really need to converse with you."

She shyly responded from her dream state, "I don't believe we've been properly introduced, sir," then looked down in embarrassment.

He apologized politely for his rudeness, and then said, "I am Captain Daniel Sutherland of the 27th Connecticut Company, and I really do need to speak with you."

Lindy was moving in and out of her dream state now, and when she raised her head again, he was gone. Dreaming, she began to rush through a forest trying to find him, but no matter where she turned, there was no sign of him. Still asleep, she began to toss in bed, and then something happened that brought her to consciousness. Her bed most assuredly moved as if someone had sat down.

Again she heard his voice. "Miss Lindy, I need to talk to you."

She slowly opened her eyes, and there at the end of her bed was the officer from the curio shop. Certain now that she was still dreaming, she propped herself up on her elbow and courteously said, "Where did you go, sir?"

However, when the deep male voice began to respond back, "Hello ..." Lindy started to panic, as she slowly began to realize that she was no longer dreaming. Too frightened to scream, she pulled the sheets over her nose and she stared in disbelief.

Upon seeing her terror, the Captain jumped off the bed and rolled backwards, passing right through the wall. As he stuck his head back through the partition to try to console her, the sight of a head poking out of a wall was too much for Lindy to handle, and she fainted dead away.

The light of daybreak embraced her as she slowly opened her eyes. She looked all around her room to see if anything was out of place, certain that her memory of the night's encounter was only a hallucination. Comfortable that all was where it should be, she chuckled that such a dream could make her behave so foolishly. "If it was a dream?" she quickly wondered to herself.

Lindy made herself jump out of bed and get into the shower; she knew that Jane would be calling her soon to get started for the day. Having just lathered up, she heard a frighteningly familiar male voice say, "I need to speak to you ... and explain about last night"

"Where are you?" she screamed. "Who are you? How did you get in here? What do you want? Get out of here!"

"Please let me explain, ma'am," the ghostly voice implored from right outside the shower door.

Lindy opened the door ever so slightly, saw the handsome officer and screamed again, "Get out of my bathroom!" She quickly rinsed off, grabbed her bathrobe, and stormed into the bedroom. Lindy had moved beyond fear into anger, and she was ready to get physical if necessary with this intruder. But as she was entering the room, Lindy found herself passing abruptly right through the officer. She took a swing then at the Captain, and watched as her fist moved right through him. In amazement she realized that this trespasser was actually a ghost, a real ghost. She began to get woozy and sat down on her bed.

The Captain stood quietly, hoping that his demeanor would relieve some of her fear. He was right. After a moment she stood up bravely and looked right at him, and demanded, "Are you a ghost?" Then, "You *are* a ghost! My God! What do you want with me?"

Captain Daniel Sutherland tried to introduce himself again to Lindy, but didn't get too far. There was a banging on the door, and Lindy's girlfriend Jane was screaming, "Are you all right?" Then she demanded entry into the small bedroom.

Lindy, feeling a little better, politely turned to the Captain and said calmly, "Excuse me a moment." She moved from the bed and opened the door for her friend.

Jane, looking all around, then said, "What's going on? What was all that screaming?" Confused at not seeing her girlfriend in any distress and alone, Jane asked her, "Lindy, what were you hollering about?"

Lindy evenly responded, "*He's* what I'm yelling about," as she pointed to the Captain. Jane looked at the empty space Lindy's finger addressed, and then gave her friend a puzzled yet concerned look. Recognizing her friend's confusion, Lindy turned to the Captain and said, "She can't see you, can she?" The Captain shook his head.

"See who?" Jane demanded.

"HIM!" Lindy pointed again.

"Him *who*?" Jane questioned, beginning to get very worried about her friend.

The Captain said, "I can get her to see me, ma'am, but please have her sit down in case she's not quite ready to handle it."

Lindy, who was feeling more comfortable with the apparition with every passing minute, turned to her friend and said, "Remember how I promised you that if I saw anything unusual, I'd let you know? ... Well, you'd better sit down because there's something I want to share with you. I think you're gonna like this." Then Lindy smiled broadly.

Jane looked perplexed as she slowly sat down on the bed and then made a gesture with her hands that appeared to ask, "*Well? What?*"

Lindy turned back to the Captain and said, "Well?"

He closed his eyes tightly and concentrated. Jane's eyes got bigger as the Captain's image began to become clear. She rubbed them quickly and then shrieked happily, *"OH MY GOD!"* Her voice trembling as she rambled on. "I knew there were ghosts ... I knew it ... I knew it ... I just knew it!"

Lindy turned to the Captain and said calmly, "Thank you, Captain. This is my very best friend Jane. Jane, this is Captain Daniel ... what did you say your last name was?"

"Sutherland, ma'am."

They greeted each other, and then the girls just stared. Lindy then sat down near her friend, and together they looked in amazement at the ghost. The Captain could see they weren't in any condition to carry on a conversation. Besides, he realized he needed to purge his aching soul, so without further delay he began the story of the tragic tale that he'd held inside for 136 years.

"I died on July the second, 1863. I didn't mind dying for my country. I believed in trying to preserve the Union, and knew that the ultimate sacrifice was a real possibility." The Captain's expression grew distressed as he continued. "But it was the news I received *before* my death that I just couldn't comprehend. One of the young boys, Jedidiah

Montgomery, came to the camp directly from my hometown of Huntington Connecticut, he brought me news that I had been listed as dead three months earlier, and that my fiancée Sarah—my life, my heart—had married my dear friend Thomas Paine not very long after she heard the news. It just doesn't make sense to me. It's not that I fault her for marrying. Part of me is thankful she was able to go on without me. But I couldn't believe she would do it so *quickly* … so I have been suspended in this room for all these years, reviewing the information over and over in my mind, just trying to make some sense of it, but I just can't."

Then he turned to Lindy and smiled. She smiled back. He looked deep into her eyes and said, "When the door opened two days ago and you walked in, I thought I was looking into the eyes of my Sarah. Your resemblance to her is remarkable. She was my reason for living from the moment I was blessed with the sight of her."

The Captain proceeded to tell his tale. "I met her quite by accident one afternoon while buying dry goods for my parents' farm. We were both quite young at the time. When she walked past me our eyes met, and I knew that I must meet her. In that first instant, I felt my feet leave the ground. Butterflies danced in my stomach as I noticed how her soft blue eyes glistened from the sun's reflection through the windowpane of the country store. Her voice, like music, echoed in my ears. I attempted to act sophisticated as I introduced myself to her. But I am quite sure I sounded as if I was stumbling over every word as they moved recklessly past my lips. She told me her name was Sarah Elizabeth McKee. She had just arrived from Boston with her family.

"We soon began to see each other regularly, as I would come up with any excuse to ride out to her place. Her father was a banker, and so I made myself available to do repairs around their farm, like fixing fences and repairing front porch steps. One day after a month of doing odd jobs,

Sarah invited me to a fried chicken picnic lunch she had prepared for us. We rode out in their buggy to the pasture. She laid out a blanket under a large oak tree as I retrieved the picnic basket. Then I turned toward her and, found myself staring at the most beautiful face God had ever created, I placed my hands on that face and told her I was going to kiss her. She resisted ever so weakly as my lips touched hers. I immediately felt a part of her letting go. She kissed me back ever so softly, and I was shaking with emotion as I felt our two hearts becoming one. I knew in that instant that we would forever be joined, regardless of the time and space that might come between us. Her touch told me for certain that we would never be the same again.

We vowed that very moment to begin courting, and that when the time was right, I would ask her father for her hand in marriage. My best friend Thomas was the only person at the time that I could confide in, so I spilled out my heart to him, described how very kind and beautiful she was and how much I loved her. He said after meeting her that I was the luckiest guy alive. Needless to say, I agreed with him.

"The three of us were inseparable over the years. We went on town picnics and to dances together. We finished all our basic schooling together, and were pretty much always only a stone's throw from one another.

It wasn't until Thomas got injured from a fall off his horse that things changed. Thank God I found him that afternoon or he could have died. The doc said the pressure of the horse's weight had caused some bad injuries and swelling on the inside of his leg and that the damage would never go away." Daniel swallowed and continued, "Thomas kept to himself after that and didn't much smile anymore. Sarah and I would try to get him to join us, but he said he would just slow us down. Also after that, things between Sarah and me got more intense, and our feelings for each other were reaching a fever's pitch. I wanted us to start a life together—but life got in our way a little.

"My Pa had passed away, and it fell on my brother Benjamin and me to take over the farm and all the responsibilities that it involved. Benjamin knew I wanted to continue my schooling, and one day in the fields he said, 'Daniel, you've always been better at learning than I ever was, and it would be good for you to get an education and bring back ideas that would help us make the farm more productive.' Then he put his arm around my shoulder and said, 'I love you, little brother, and I want you to make us proud.'

"My plan was to go to college and then come back and marry Sarah. I wasn't sure how she would feel about my being away, but when I told her, she smiled and said, 'I will write you everyday.' So I went to the university and sure enough, she wrote me every day. I made it home most weekends and every vacation.

"After my graduation from Harvard, I went to her father and asked for his daughter's hand in marriage. He knew how his daughter felt about me and gave his blessing. Sarah and I announced to all our friends and family our engagement. We spent many evenings then, talking about the upcoming marriage and our life together.

"However, the sounds of war were growing all around us and I knew that before we could tie the knot, I would be called to service to do my part to preserve the Union. Sure enough, on April the twelfth, 1861, everything changed. Shots were fired on Fort Sumter in Charleston Harbor, and I felt compelled to enlist in the militia.

"When I was commissioned a 2nd Lieutenant, Sarah was there. I don't believe there was a prouder person in the world as we walked down the main street of Huntington. I was her hero and could do no wrong. As word came from my unit that I would soon be called to duty, Sarah and I discussed what we should do. I told her again how I felt about preserving the Union and that I was convinced that the war would last just a few months. Surely we could wait till then.

"Sarah kissed me gently and said, 'you are right, my love—a few months, and then we will have forever.' She went and had one of those new fangled pictures made, then had a lock of her hair, woven ever so intricately, placed on the other side of the photograph. Sarah had the picture placed in a CdV with the picture of her facing out and an engraving on the back, which read, 'Beloved.'"

Jane could see that Lindy didn't understand what a CdV was so, after quickly apologizing to the Captain for interrupting she interjected, "A CdV was usually a picture card that was given to a soldier from a loved one, to be kept close to his heart."

Lindy thanked her girlfriend without taking her eyes off Daniel Sutherland as he again took up his story.

He turned, facing Lindy, and began to speak about Sarah and their incredible resemblance. "You are so very much like her. The moment you walked through the door, I found myself wanting to move again, to feel again, and to love again! Through all this time I still love my Sarah, as if I had said goodbye only a moment ago."

As he said the words, "I still love my Sarah," Lindy had to wipe tears from her cheeks. How she longed for someone to look at her just this way and say these words to her.

Daniel then proceeded to speak of his last night together with Sarah. He looked at both the ladies and apologized to them in advance if what he was about to say would embarrass either of them, though he felt somehow that it would not. His eyes moved downward as he began to relive that night.

"We knew it would be the last time we saw each other for some time, and we decided without hesitation not to share ourselves with anyone else on our last evening together. We planned how we would conduct our long-distance relationship, and said all the things that needed saying one more time. It's funny, now that I'm dead, I can recall every single word that was spoken that night—and much was said. Sarah looked deep into my eyes and spoke:

> *"From the moment our eyes met, I knew deep within my soul that you and I were meant to be together forever. I have become resolute that my stomach will do flips every time I see or even think of you, and I am sure you have noticed the movement of my hand to my abdomen every time you greet me.*
>
> *However, ever since word came of your imminent departure, this feeling of which I speak has been accompanied by an aching of my heart unlike anything I have ever known. I mourn for you, though I know for now you are still within my reach.*
>
> *Daniel, my love, if there are to be but a few hours before your leaving, I need you to touch me. I need you to possess me with unbridled passion, the passion I know you have restrained for countless years. For if I am to be alone even for just a few months, or God knows how long, I beg you, leave with me a memory that can sustain me—and, my darling, a memory that will sustain you as well."*

"Our emotions were running high, and we spent much of the time that evening wiping the tears from each other's eyes. I don't know exactly at what moment we fell into a passionate embrace, but once locked into it, there was no letting go. Our kisses were wet and wild as our lips pressed together and then moved all over our faces. I couldn't stop my hands as they moved beneath her blouse, cupping the breasts that I had only dreamed of touching over the past twelve years. I was lost as the smell of her

71

filled my head. Our clothes seemed to remove themselves frantically, and we drew close together, flesh against flesh, bodies moving in rhythm. As I looked down upon her, I was brought to tears by her beauty, and one by one my tears fell upon her breasts and neck. Each teardrop made her sob almost uncontrollably knowing that within a few hours I might be gone...forever. Exhausted, we held each other as the sweat from our bodies chilled us. Sleep tried to overtake us, but the realization that these were our last moments made even the thought of resting impossible. We moved again into each other's embrace trying to get inside one another's skin, sure that being together was where we belonged."

Daniel put his head down as his feelings had gotten the better of him. His eyes filled with tears. He raised his head up and said, "I don't understand...I just don't!" And in that instant he was gone from the room.

The girls looked at each other first in astonishment at what they had both just experienced, then in deep melancholy, as the Captain's story of love related to both of them—Jane because of the great love she had lost, and Lindy for never having found love at all.

Chapter Seven

Lindy and Jane must have looked at each other, speechless, for what seemed like hours. When they were able to speak again, the room was filled with "Oh, my God!"

Finally, Lindy turned to her friend, silent tears falling from her face. "What a tortured soul." Jane nodded to her friend.

Lindy wiped her face with her robe and replied, "A tortured soul that needs our help."

"What can we do to help him?" Jane asked her friend inquisitively.

Lindy thought for a minute, "There must be more information about the Captain in one of the museums, or in the local library."

"Well, if spirits walk the earth because of unresolved lives, and Daniel's life sure sounds unresolved, maybe we can help him find the answers he needs to move on to the next plane and, better yet, to find Sarah," Jane said with confidence.

"What are we waiting for?" Lindy announced as she jumped from her bed and headed for the door. Then just before leaving, she realized she was wearing only a bathrobe. She shrugged her shoulders, then turned to her friend and said, "Let me get dressed real fast."

"Good idea, Lin." Jane giggled. With that the two girls dressed in historical fashion and headed for the Gettysburg Museum.

Once inside the museum, Lindy recalled that the Captain had received a CdV from Sarah. Since he was dead, perhaps it was among the many personal belongings on display in the main room. She relayed her thoughts to Jane.

Her girlfriend turned to a handsome official with curly black hair, who wore a ranger's outfit...His name badge read *Ranger Jimmy*. Jane was glad for an excuse to strike up a conversation. She asked him if there were personal effects, and such, in the museum.

Jimmy looked down at the beauty standing in front of him and stammered, "You might find those artifacts in the glass cases three rooms down, ma'am."

Jane's eyes lit up at the officer as she smiled back, "Thanks, Jimmy."

Lindy was already moving from one glass case to another. Jane thought to ask her friend how they would know it was the Captain's memorabilia, and then realized that they must look for anything with a picture of Lindy on it.

Jimmy watched the two women as they searched the cases, apparently looking for something. Row after row they searched, looking for any picture that might remotely look like Lindy. Then, as Lindy turned a corner, she saw Jane staring at the case in front of her. Lindy hesitated for a moment, as she stood halfway down the aisle. Jane had become pale.

Lindy quickly walked over and caught her breath with a gasp. "My God," she whispered as she put her hand to her mouth. Lindy found that she was looking at the very image she had seen in her own mirror the night before. Even the pulled-up hair was exactly as Lindy had worn it. Then she saw engraved on the silver case the word, *'BELOVED.'* The case also contained a belt buckle, a holster, a revolver, and a small note card that said:

'Captain Daniel Sutherland, Shelton (previously Huntington), Connecticut, hero of the Wheatfield engagement, killed in action, July 2nd 1863, of multiple gun shot wounds.'

The girls were unsure what this might mean to the Captain, but they decided to return to Lindy's room in hopes that their discovery might be able to help him. Jimmy the ranger noted their departure as they scrambled for the door. He sighed, catching a brief glimpse of the dark-haired, lovely woman.

On arriving inside her room, Lindy called out the Captain's name, "Captain! ... Captain Sutherland!" but the room remained silent. She felt a chill move through her and was sure he must be close by, so she called to him again, "Captain!" The two sat in the room for a while without a response. "Where do you think he's gone?" Lindy turned to Jane.

"Maybe he won't come back. You know, sometimes a spirit tells his terrible story and then waits for someone new, and tells the same story over and over again for all time," Jane said solemnly as she stared into Lindy's eyes.

Lindy stared back at her friend, "You've been watching too many movies." Lindy then continued, "Let's get something to eat."

Jane replied, "That's a good idea." The two friends got up and left the room.

Lindy had been right to call his name as the coldness found her. It was the Captain. He was so embarrassed after revealing the contents of what was in his heart that he could not bring himself to appear as the girls moved around the room. As he made contact with Lindy, he instantly knew where they had been, and that he must go to the museum, in hopes that whatever was found would bring him peace.

His desire for an answer moved him through stone and glass as he made his way to the museum. Once there, as he hovered above the glass cases, he found the photograph of his Sarah. Moving down to the front of the clear cabinet, Daniel stared at the woman he loved letting his fingers move through the glass to try to touch the gift that had brought him so much comfort through the arduous years of the war. His eyes moved to the print that accompanied the artifacts, where he read about himself.

He noticed, in passing, that his hometown of Huntington was now called Shelton. He realized then that his efforts on the battlefield had aided his troops in defeating General Lee's forces. The document called him a "hero," but he could only recall the frightened, young faces of the gallant men he had led into battle. He thought to himself, "*They* are the true heroes of Gettysburg." However, he found no answers within the case, and the information and the image of Sarah's incredibly beautiful face brought tears—that would never find their way to the ground as they, like him, were lost in the void of his existence.

* * *

Just after noon, having finished a delicious lunch of home-style fixings, the girls were exiting the restaurant as a familiar face appeared in the distance. Jane hit her friend lightly as she noticed him coming toward them.

The ranger, who was also the curator of the museum, had been watching them from the corner of the restaurant. When he approached them, he quietly said, "Hi, remember me?"

Jane smiled. "Hi, Jimmy. I'm Jane, and this is Lindy."

He nodded respectfully. "Hi, Jane," he said, unable to take his eyes off her. "Are you two interested in seeing some of the artifacts that aren't on display?"

"What kind of memorabilia do you have, Jimmy?" Jane inquired, smiling. Lindy, smiling to herself, watched Jane go to work on the ranger.

"There are ledgers and books regarding some of the goings-on here. You two appear to be looking for something in particular … what might it be?"

Not wishing to declare that a ghostly spirit had visited them, the girls indicated that they had heard stories about a certain Captain Daniel Sutherland. Upon hearing the name, the ranger's eyebrows went straight up, indicating to the girls that it wasn't the first time he had heard the name.

Jane thought to herself, "He must know something more." Jane astonished her girlfriend as she sauntered closer to the tall, handsome figure, and proceeded to seduce him with her charms. He became like putty in her hands as she questioned him about the Captain.

Jimmy said, "I know of a book written about Captain Sutherland around the turn of the century by a little-known author named Jeb or Jed Montgomery; I'm not sure which."

Lindy's mouth fell open, recognizing the name, as Jane pursued the topic further. "Do you have the book in the museum?" she asked ever so sweetly.

"No, but I think I might be able to find you a copy at the public library. It's filled with old books about the Civil War and many of the battles that were fought here." Then, before Jane could even ask, he added, "We do have some of the letters that were written to the Captain by his fiancée."

As the curator said the word "fiancée," he turned toward Lindy, suddenly recognizing her resemblance to the CdV in the museum. Unable to stop gazing at Lindy, Jimmy had started to comment on her similarity to the picture, when Jane boldly interrupted him and asked if they might get a peek at the letters.

Ranger Jimmy continued staring at Lindy …, "If you come by tomorrow at noon, I'll make them available to you."

With a light touch, Jane turned his head away from Lindy and, looking deeply into his eyes, held his chin with her fingers and said, "You're just the sweetest man, Jimmy! I'll see *you* tomorrow." She accented her walk as they left the attractive man flustered by her obvious and sincere manipulation. Jane turned to Lindy and said, "This is turning out to be the best trip to Gettysburg I've ever had."

After dark, as Daniel slowly made his way back to his 136-year-old residence, he had a very eerie encounter. There on the streets of Gettysburg was a soldier whom he thought he recognized. He moved closer and then passed through the person; he quickly fell back. "Samuel Paine?" He thought. "That's kinda strange..." He moved, more slowly the second time, toward the stranger and made another pass through. "...from Shelton, Connecticut?" Daniel took two steps away and then remembered the town's name change. He turned and made contact again, "Why is God doing this to me?" Meanwhile images were moving through his head, images that were somehow familiar to him. He noticed his energy was rapidly becoming depleted. He wanted to know why this stranger's memories seemed to be somehow intertwining with his own, but was unable to muster up the strength to make another pass. Daniel thought to himself, "How much unhappiness was in the heart of this Samuel Paine?" He remained motionless as the familiar stranger continued walking in the darkness.

Meanwhile Samuel Paine moved slowly down the street, rubbing his arms, curious about the fleeting moments of coldness he had just experienced. He was quite unaware of his close encounter with the Gettysburg ghost.

Timothy, the rebel, approached the paralyzed spirit he had encountered by Devil's Den and said with a laugh, "Are we learning, Captain?" Daniel could only listen as Timothy continued to taunt the officer. "You'll wear yourself out by running into the living. That's why most of us just move things around." Daniel looked beyond Timothy's shoulder as half-visible spirits made their way in and out of the town. "By the way you look, I'd say you were better off in your room. You're not going to get answers from any of these mortals; they're just tourists visiting a battlefield." With that, Timothy flew up and over Daniel and vanished into the night.

Daniel, still petrified from his latest encounter with the living, stood alone on one of the historic streets of Gettysburg, forced to ponder what his ghostly adversary had warned. "I wish Timothy would just leave me alone," he decided. "What more could happen anyway? I'm already dead."

Then he thought of the new stranger in the street. Who was this character and what, if anything, did he have to do with what was happening to him? Was there no sense, no meaning, in this existence between Heaven and Earth?

His heart ached endlessly for his Sarah. He missed her smile, her voice, and the touch of her lips on his. Yet every time he encountered Lindy Dennison, he was obligated to feel the pain again. "Why has she come here?" he thought to himself. Daniel knew from his brief contacts with her that she had never really known love, or even had a firsthand understanding of what it could be like. Could this be part of God's plan for him? If he could somehow help her find or at least understand love, would he be released from his earthly prison? Why else would he be able to get information from the living? "There must be a connection," he contemplated. As his strength slowly came back to him, he moved with more determination. "If there is a way to get out of here, I'm going to find it."

The "Beloved Captain" realized that he could no longer live through eternity as a silent spectator. His walk became determined as he made his way back to his resting place. With each step he became surer that Lindy was the key. Somehow he must help her to find the precious emotion that had eluded her thus far, and the only way to do that was to explore her life for answers.

Daniel moved silently through the door to his room, which was being occupied by a sleeping vision of pure loveliness. He stared at every detail of her lovely, familiar face. Suddenly, without a thought to the consequences,

Daniel entered Lindy as she slept. His spirit felt a shock of electricity as he moved into her subconscious. He felt as if he were falling though water and moving blindly toward muffled sounds.

Then Daniel found himself in a very dark corridor that twisted to the left and to the right. Both sides of the crooked hallway were stacked with crates, and each container seemed to be emitting sounds. As Daniel moved closer to the carton nearest him, he was suddenly pulled through its wall. He found himself standing in a small, darkened bedroom decorated in pink colors with pretty flowered wallpaper. It was a child's room. The sounds he heard were coming from a tiny little girl who was lying across the bed, crying. He thought to himself, "This must be Lindy."

He moved closer to the child's bed and softly asked, "Are you all right, Lindy?"

The little girl rubbed her eyes as she slowly lifted her head. "Who are you?" she asked politely as she tried to catch her breath.

"I'm Daniel," he replied. "Why are you crying so?" he questioned gently.

"My daddy left me and my mommy and it's my entire fault," she whimpered.

"I don't think so, sweetheart. What makes you say that?" Daniel inquired compassionately.

"I didn't clean my room good enough." She began to weep again.

Daniel sat on the edge of her bed, and she instinctively moved into his arms. "It had nothing to do with you, darling, nothing at all," the Captain assured her. He rocked her as she continued to cry, until the tiny angel finally fell asleep. Daniel carefully placed her under the covers and kissed her cheek.

Then he moved near his entrance point and fell from the crate to the floor of the dark passageway. "These boxes must contain Lindy's memories," he thought to himself. Then: "Are these the barriers and walls I encountered when I first made contact with her?" Daniel's question was about to be answered as he moved into another container.

Daniel's eyes took a moment to adjust as he noticed that the walls of the pretty pink bedroom had grown somewhat discolored with age. His attention moved quickly to a tall, dark figure moving toward the bed where an older Lindy lay sleeping. The figure squatted down, and then slipped his hand under the young girl's sheets. Her eyes opened and flashed with fear, as she pleaded quietly, "Daddy Charles, please don't ... please."

Daniel pushed the crouching man to the floor. The man got up and looked around the darkened room. Although he saw nothing, his expression was one of fear as he quickly departed. Lindy looked over and asked, "Are you Daniel?"

The Captain nodded as he questioned, "Who was that?"

Lindy answered, "That's my stepfather. He touches me in my private places. I don't like it. I don't like him, he scares me. He didn't see you, did he, because he can get very mad sometimes?"

"No, he didn't," Daniel answered. Then his piercing blue-green eyes made contact with Lindy's eyes. "Lindy, you are not responsible for what he's doing, and you must tell your mother what he's been doing to you. Do you understand?" She sensed that it was essential for her to obey him.

"I will, Daniel ... I promise," she replied earnestly.

He moved near her and placed his large palm lightly against her cheek. Then he told her softly, "Everything will be all right. You need to believe that." She stared at the soldier and believed him. As he moved away from her, she waved, and then he disappeared through the faded-flower wall.

Daniel found himself on the ground outside the box. As he got back up on his feet, Daniel noticed something very strange. Some of the large crates had begun to vanish into nothingness. He thought to himself, "Could I be making a difference? I can't stop the bad things from happening to her, so what's the use?" Still he moved forward. Daniel was sure that the corridor in which he stood was a chronicle of Lindy's past. He felt helpless as he scanned the multitude of boxes that still surrounded him. "How could she begin to know love with a past of such rejection and abuse?" Daniel began to get frustrated as he slowly walked down the footpath through the maze of her subconscious. He paused in front of one enclosure as a familiar voice echoed from the other side.

"Oh, my God!" Lindy was shrieking in disbelief, as Daniel moved through the barrier that divided them. Her attention was directed away from Daniel toward a corner of what appeared to be a library. A teenaged boy was showing a lot of interest in a girl of about the same age. As his lips touched the girl's, a tear appeared, but refused to fall, from Lindy's adolescent face.

Daniel watched and then asked, without taking his eyes off the intimate couple, "Who is that?"

Lindy recognized the voice and responded with anger, "It was my boyfriend!"

The Captain realized that he had become more than just an observer in her life, and he could tell that right now she needed some words of encouragement. They turned towards each other as he said softly, "It's okay to cry when someone hurts you, you know."

She responded fiercely, *"No one is going to hurt me again; I won't let them get that close."*

The Captain knew in his heart that Lindy would never know true happiness unless she could allow herself to be exposed to all the possibilities love might offer, but he just said in a matter-of-fact way, "You will get hurt again, and maybe again after that, until one day love finds you. You'll need to keep your eyes open."

She watched closely as he moved backwards through the wall and disappeared. Daniel continued to walk down the path until he came upon a large box that had a male voice emanating from it. He slipped through its wall and found himself standing behind Lindy. Her live-in boyfriend, John, was confessing to a multitude of infidelities.

She asked him why, her face flushed with emotion. He told her he had never loved her. Lindy was devastated. She demanded to know more.

"I never had fun with you. You were a prude, and you never satisfied me. Does that answer your damn question?" John screamed at her as he grabbed his suitcases and jerked open the screen door.

Lindy began to cry, trying hard to hold the tears back. "I won't give him the satisfaction," she thought to herself.

Daniel's hand found her shoulder. He squeezed gently and said, "This isn't love, Lindy. Love is patient and love is kind. It makes you feel like butterflies are flying in your stomach. Somebody real smart told me that a long time ago. So don't ever lose hope, because as long as you have hope, the door to love will be open. I promise." Then instantly he fell backwards through the wall.

He continued to move through the water-like channel his body bombarded with electrical impulses. The shock waves increased with greater intensity as he found himself reversing his path down the corridor of her memories and exiting her subconscious. He collapsed to the floor, exhausted and totally unable to move. His body seemed chilled to the bone, though he was dead and had no true sense of hot and cold, it caused him to quake out of control. He curled up by Lindy's bed, attempting to watch her as she slept, but he was trembling so intensely that he was reduced to a shaking heap, silently thrashing on the wooden floor beside her bed. For the first time in over a century, Daniel was really frightened, for he had a gut reaction that he might fade into nothingness. Hours seemed to pass before he could manage a full thought. He considered what impact his entry into her subconscious might have had on this beauty that had brought him out of his eternal purgatory. He had a feeling of accomplishment that he hadn't had since he walked the earth—but at what price, he wondered, as he continued to shake violently.

Chapter Eight

Sarah began to scream uncontrollably as the devastating news crossed over Thomas Paine's lips. Nothing could have prepared her for the total devastation that pierced through her heart. Daniel and she had talked of the dangers of war and the possibility that he might not return, but she always felt that the love she had for him would in some way keep him from harm and bring him home. Lost were the dreams of their life together as she hugged herself and slumped helplessly to the ground, unable to handle the horrible news of her Daniel's death.

Thomas nervously helped her to the front porch swing. He could do nothing but watch as her mother held her while she trembled and convulsed, wailing the death cry that had become all too common across the country as the war waged on.

After that fateful visit Thomas came every morning over the next few weeks, bringing soup from a local establishment and wildflowers he picked along the way, and tried to assist Sarah's family as they stood watch over her. They took turns force-feeding her, as she remained nearly comatose at the loss of her one true love.

Day after day, her dear mother tried to console Sarah, "You must be strong, Sarah. Daniel would be distraught to see you this way." But the mere mention of his name sent her into hysteria.

Each morning Thomas would come by and sit with her, sometimes not saying anything at all. They were all concerned that if she did not begin to recover, her own death would soon follow.

For her part, Sarah tried with all her heart to find closure, but there could be no end for her because, unbeknownst to Thomas, there was a secret she had not revealed to anyone. Her realization came during the second week of her mourning, for as she lay upon the bed, something began to move deep within her abdomen. She didn't move a muscle, yet a wiggle seemed to pass from one side to the other. It was then that she knew that Daniel had left a part of himself behind, a living reminder of his eternal love...

Aware that her health was in jeopardy, suddenly and without warning, she got out of bed and began to make breakfast for the entire household. When Thomas arrived at the house, he was flabbergasted at her behavior. He looked around the table at her family, who looked as shocked as he did. Emily, Sarah's mother, just looked over at Thomas and motioned him to sit at the table.

"Sarah," he finally said, "You're up! I can scarcely believe it."

She responded in a matter-of-fact way, "Life goes on, Thomas, as must I. Would you like some coffee?" He nodded as he found a seat at the table, dumbfounded at the change in her.

After breakfast, when all had gone about their business, Sarah called her mother to the parlor and revealed the truth, trusting that her mother would know what to do. Mother Emily, well aware of Thomas' desires, told her daughter what she should consider and what she might expect for her child if it were discovered that the baby was a bastard. Together they decided that their secret would remain just that. Thomas would never know the truth, because she feared that he might reject her, if he knew she was carrying Daniel's baby and that she had been with him illicitly. There could be no other course of action, and although her heart was still centered on her Daniel, she knew that for her child, Thomas would be his father in only six months.

Thomas Paine wasted no time in courting Sarah. He was somewhat surprised at her willingness to allow it so rapidly after the horrible news of Daniel. He was dubious at her return of affections, but paid no heed to his trepidation.

For above all else, Thomas feared she might in some way discover his treachery, the awful lie that was already torturing his soul. He thought to himself, "God forgive me for what I have done." He was in anguish. But he also assured himself thinking, "There is no way for anyone to know what I have done, I'm almost sure of it."

His fears began to manifest themselves in the form of nightmares. Images of a lone horseman in a blue Union uniform, sword drawn, chased him through the night as he tried desperately to get away. Thomas was finding it harder and harder to sleep as he recoiled in terror at such images and at possible discovery of his deception—for his best friend, Daniel Sutherland, the one who saved his leg as a young boy, was not dead at all.

Thomas had plotted the ultimate deceit after suffering years and years of jealousy over the relationship of Daniel and Sarah. For the past year, Thomas had been responsible for contacting the families of the fallen soldiers. He knew that the battle statistics were becoming more dismal. Each monthly report that the Huntington Post Office received showed increasing numbers of fatalities from the battlefields. He had been looking over each list as it arrived, and he cursed himself when he found himself praying to find Daniel's name among the fallen.

Thomas slowly began to hatch his plan. As the only person entrusted with the names of the dead and informing the families, he was in the perfect position to carry out his fraud. One day he very simply placed Daniel's name on the directory of the dead. Understanding that Sarah would fall to pieces, he planned to be right there to console her through the grieving process, and then when the time was right, he would ask her to be his wife. After all, he reasoned to himself, she had already waited too long to be wed by Daniel, and now there was no reason to wait any longer.

As the Postmaster, he reminded himself that, he alone knew the names of the deceased; there would be no one to question him. If Daniel should live through the conflict, his arrival would be much too late. His death would be seen as a clerical error and nothing more. Thomas knew Daniel to be an honorable man. He would be forced to go away rather than stand by as the woman he loved passed each day in the arms of another, even if the other person was his best friend.

"Anyway," rationalized Thomas, "if Daniel loved her so very much, why did he make her wait so long to be wed?" Thomas silently cursed himself each time he caught his reflection in the mirror, but he forgot everything of his evil plan, when the thought of Sarah came into his mind's eye.

His fiendish plot had worked all too well. As the first month of her mourning reached its end, Thomas and Sarah announced their engagement.

On the day of the wedding, before saying her vows, Sarah Elizabeth McKee sat in the garden and sent a silent message to Heaven. She declared that no matter what happened or whom she would be with, it could be nothing more than make-believe, for in her heart there was only room for Daniel Sutherland.

An hour later, the bells of the church were ringing for the newlyweds. The town folk applauded Thomas for his kindness and his willingness to help Sarah get on with her life. Not only did he get his heart's desire, he also gained a new found respect in the community. From that day forward Thomas would become a leader in the township, a man of honor.

Baby Thomas Paine, Junior, was born on the thirty-first of December in the year of the Gettysburg Battle. He had Sarah's eyes, and Thomas was so very proud he could barely contain himself. As the couple strolled down Main

Street, they were stopped repeatedly by friends and neighbors who commented how very beautiful the young boy was, and how quickly he was growing despite his premature arrival. Any rumors soon dissipated as concerns about the war were increasingly on the lips of the citizens of Huntington. The North was finally wearing down the South, and wounded soldiers were returning home, replaced by young men eager to show their patriotism.

The younger Thomas was sixteen months old when General Robert E. Lee surrendered to General Ulysses S. Grant at Appomattox on April the ninth, 1865. He was on the street with his mother and father, waving a small American flag when word reached the town. Guns were going off, the town band was playing *The Battle Hymn of the Republic*, and *When Johnny comes Marching Home* with everyone cheering and celebrating.

Thomas Paine, Junior, grew tall and strong as the years went by. He proved to have a keen mind and a physically powerful appearance, with broad shoulders and long, wavy black hair. The years moved by all too quickly for Sarah as she watched her child grow into manhood.

Thomas, Junior, was very interested in farming, drawn to the rich dark soil of his Connecticut birthplace. This was a major disappointment to his father, who had been making other plans for his one and only son.

Thomas, Senior, had been instrumental politically in the development of the Ousatonic Water Company, which created a dam that led to the creation of a new downtown area. Edward Shelton, the president of the water company, was more than honored when, through Thomas Paine's influence, Huntington was renamed Shelton. Having established the Paine name as an advocate for the betterment of Shelton, the elder Thomas had always hoped his namesake would become a lawyer and run for public office.

Father and son would argue all the time as young Thomas moved from adolescence into adulthood. "I've laid out a red carpet for you, son. This town would elect you to any position you wish, even mayor, in a heartbeat."

"It's not for me, Father. I only feel at home when my hands are full of rich Huntington soil."

His father corrected him sternly, "You mean Shelton soil."

"It might be Shelton to you and Mr. Shelton, but for me his assisting the community doesn't justify changing the name of the town that has been Huntington all our lives! Is that how you secure power for yourself, by giving away what isn't even yours?"

His father angrily slapped him across the face. The son stood staring at his father with clenched fists, then turned and stormed out of the house. He got on his horse and rode away into the night.

A few days later, young Thomas approached his mother. "I can't be what he wants me to be just because it's part of his grand plan for me." Thomas continued, "He has never asked me what would make me happy. He doesn't even care."

Sarah always knew that once her son got all of his anger out, he would be all right. She listened thoughtfully as young Thomas told her, "I know I'm a giant disappointment to father. He's never been happy with my choices." Tom tried to explain to his mother. "Ma, my plans are just not his, and you've always told me to follow my heart."

Sarah said, "Your father is proud of the person you've become, and he knows down deep that you must follow your own dreams."

The two men finally resolved their differences, neither apologizing for what had happened. Thomas Paine finally accepted the fact that his son was destined to be a farmer. So for his twenty-first birthday, he gave his son twenty acres of land adjacent to their farm.

When young Thomas found himself a wife, Jenny Wilcott, Sarah knew that she was the one. Jenny was a warm soul from a loving family and appeared to love Thomas desperately. Thomas had long been enchanted with Jenny. For Sarah, their mutual love was all that mattered. Two years later the couple brought a son, Joshua, into the world. Sarah loved the baby almost as if she had carried him herself.

Joshua loved his grandma Sarah and spent long hours with her from the beginning. She read him stories of America's recent struggle, adding stories about a gallant Captain on a mighty chestnut steed, which almost always brought her to the brink of tears.

On those occasions, Joshua would look up and say, "Don't cry, Grandma. I'll take care of you, I promise." At that she would look down and smile a proud smile.

In the summer of 1899, the elder Thomas had taken severely ill and was bed ridden. One day he called his wife into their bedroom. Thomas was aware of the gravity of his affliction, and felt compelled to make a final confession. He had tortured himself for so many years and tried with all his heart to be a good husband, but each time he looked deeply into her eyes, there was Daniel, proud and tall, and without the many faults that Thomas possessed. He hated himself. "Where do I start?" he weakly questioned himself out loud.

Sarah sat by his bed and told him, "Just rest easy, Tom."

Thomas Paine, however, could not rest easy; he knew that if he did not speak out quickly, an eternity of damnation of the most horrendous description awaited him. He stared at his wife … then finally spoke. "Sarah, I must tell you something that will surely make you find me insufferable. But very soon I must meet my Creator, and I cannot hold on to my treachery for another moment." He averted his eyes from Sarah's and began. "Sarah, my darling Sarah, you know how much I love you." He slowly brought his eyes to hers. "Don't you? Sarah nodded, very curious about what he might tell her.

Thomas, unsure how to start his confession, stammered and then suddenly blurted out, "I betrayed Daniel, and I deceived you." Still looking deep into his wife's eyes, he continued. "I placed Daniel's name on the list of the dead before he had died." Sarah stared in disbelief. Thomas, now spoke without hesitation. "He was not killed until the second of July in Gettysburg, 1863. I knew the battles were getting worse as the names of the dead kept increasing with each report I received. The thought of Daniel's coming home and my never being with you was more than my heart could take. I, therefore, let jealousy rule my actions."

Sarah looked intently at him, expressionless, but said not a word. There were no words for what he had done. Her husband of over thirty years was not long for this earth, and Sarah didn't know what to feel. Her face twitched slightly as she held back her tears.

Thomas felt as though he had stabbed her with a knife as he continued his declaration of guilt. "I kept all your letters to Daniel and then sent them off when I received word that he had truly died." Thomas began to cough severely. His voice getting weaker, he offered, "I can only give you one thing before I die—for you never belonged to me and I had no right ..." He coughed again. "I have Daniel's letters. They're here."

She narrowed her eyes and looked at him, somewhat confused. "Under my desk" ... He coughed. "The floor boards in my study ... the letters ... they are all there."

His eyes closed, his breathing slowed, until death found him. Thomas Paine left the earth with no secrets. As for Sarah, she felt some remorse for never really loving Thomas, the way a wife should love her husband. He had told her too much to comprehend, so she sat quietly for a time, thinking, and staring into space, then eventually covered him with a sheet.

Sarah contacted her son and broke the news to him, then made all the funeral arrangements. The Paines buried their husband and father under an oak tree that grew tall on the pasture. The service was brief. The pastor spoke of how much Thomas had given to the community, his impact on their local economy, and finally of a husband's kindness and dedication to his family. Sarah was expressionless.

Jenny suggested, "Would you like us to leave Joshua with you so you're not alone, at least for a time?"

"That would be wonderful, Jenny. Thank you for all your help." After the small reception, she kissed her son and her daughter-in-law, then waved goodbye with her grandson from the front porch as the couple rode off in their family buggy.

Sarah kept herself busy tying up loose ends and caring for Joshua. Her mind reeled each time she was near Thomas's study. "Why can't I just go in there and read those letters?" she thought at times to herself. But Sarah knew why she was apprehensive about what she might find in the letters. The thought of her beloved asking her why she hadn't written was almost too much for her to bear, and she had no way to explain to her Daniel what had happened. She must have passed the study a hundred times before she finally found the courage to go inside and look beneath the floorboards under her husband's desk.

Sarah shook with anticipation as she entered the room. She used her kitchen knife to loosen the boards, worn with age from Thomas Paine's boots as he sat at his writing desk. Sarah wondered how he could sit there day after day, knowing what was beneath him. When she finally managed to pry away the old boards, she found a rusty metal box. It was like those Thomas had used at the Post Office so many years before. The container was very heavy, and she had to use two hands to pull it out of the hole. The box was locked with a rusty metal padlock. She became somewhat frantic as she quickly looked in the hole for a key to unlock the box. She felt all around, digging into the soft dark soil with her fingernails. Her hair began to fall into her face, and she used her dirty hands to push her curls back out of the way. Sarah grunted and squealed with frustration. Then, "The desk drawer," she said out loud. Her soiled hands moved frantically through the top drawer of the desk, moving papers wildly as she became obsessed with her search. Her fingers finally made contact with something small and metal. "Thank you, God," she said as she looked at the key in her hand. Sarah fumbled slightly as she inserted the key and slowly made it turn all the way around, until the box opened. Lifting the lid, she found it brimming with letters, letters in a hauntingly familiar handwriting. She touched them gently, as if they might disintegrate if handled too harshly.

"My Daniel," she found herself saying out loud. Sarah Elizabeth McKee sat on the floor of the study where she had raised her son and read every precious word his true father had written. Although she was a grandmother, she sobbed as uncontrollably as she had done when she first received word of his death, for only now would she be able to truly mourn her soulmate. As she reached for the last letter, she trembled and slowly began to read all those beautiful words of love, scarcely able to catch her breath.

...I am unsure what is in God's plan for us. If our Lord chooses to take me in the days ahead, then I suppose that would be His will, but look not to the

glorious heavens above for me, as I shall remain close by. Instead, my darling, look for me in the summer wind that surrounds you, for I will be there embracing you as the warm wind brushes your hair.

Listen to the crackling fire as it burns brightly in your hearth, for it will be my passion for you, heating your very soul as you attempt to go through the wintry nights without me.

Look up when the spring rain falls, for it will be my lips delivering soft, wet kisses like the gentle passionate kisses of our last night together.

Finally, when your soft, blue eyes have grown weak through countless seasons in the sun, your strawberry blond hair has turned to soft silver silk lying gently across your shoulders, and the pages of my letters become too hard to read ... I will be there. And when eternity finds you and you draw your last earthly breath, fear not your departure from this world ... for I will be beside you and I will catch you as you fall.

Until forever
Daniel Sutherland

Sarah collapsed into her dress, tears falling like rain. Her grandson moved closer to her, and softly patting her head to console her, for the grief he could not truly understand.

Chapter Nine

A little over thirty years had passed, when Jedidiah Montgomery and his family got off the dusty train in Shelton, Connecticut. Everything that he had called home had become unrecognizable, including the town's name. Post-Civil War United States brought with it an age of technological advances that were changing the entire makeup of American industry. This created an increased population in urban areas, most often the poor and immigrants, to provide labor for the factories. Cobblestone-paved avenues and street lamps had replaced the country dirt roads Jedidiah had remembered. Inventors like Edison and Bell were in the newspapers, with inventions that were destined to move America into a real world power.

Jed turned to his wife of three years and said, "Things are very different, Mary. This used to be a farmland community, but now it looks like one factory after another as far as the eye can see ... very different indeed." He loaded their luggage into a buggy and headed for the hotel in town.

Mary was an attractive woman with engaging brown eyes, and she was sure Jed could do anything he set his mind on. She turned to her husband and said, "Shouldn't be too hard to find work here, whatever you have a hankering to do, Jed." Then she smiled her special smile.

Jed knew what his dear wife meant so he grinned back at her and nodded, "That's true, Mary ... that's true."

As the buggy moved down the cobbled road, Jed began to remember the past. Memories flashed into his mind as he recalled his thirty-year journey through war and peace across the vast expanse of the United States. His journey had carried him through a growing America, a country that was trying desperately to become one of united peoples regardless of race, creed, or color. Jed had thought to himself, "Maybe with the development of a growing economy, we can begin to learn to live together without so much prejudice towards one another." In his mind he recalled the day his President decreed that all men were created equal. The remembrance of that historic day clearly came into view as he recalled it ...

* * *

He had stood close to the podium in his newly cleaned uniform on November 19th, 1863. The tall presidential figure in the black suit began to speak solemnly from a speech he had started on White House stationary and completed at the Willis House the evening before ...

"Four score and seven years ago our fathers brought forth on this continent a new nation, conceived in liberty and dedicated to the proposition that all men are created equal. Now we are engaged in a great civil war, testing whether that nation or any nation so conceived and so dedicated can long endure. We are met on a great battlefield of that war. We have come to dedicate a portion of that field as a final resting-place for those who here gave their lives that that nation might live. It is altogether fitting and proper that we should do this. But in a larger sense, we cannot dedicate, we cannot consecrate, we cannot hallow this ground."

Jed's tearing eyes met the President's, as his solemn commander-in-chief continued his tribute to him and his fallen comrades.

"The brave men, living and dead, who struggled here, have consecrated it far above our poor power to add or detract. The world will little note nor long remember what we say here, but it can never forget what they did here. It is for us the living rather to be dedicated here to the unfinished work, which they who fought here have thus far so nobly advanced. It is rather for us to be here dedicated to the great task remaining before us—that from these honored dead we take increased devotion to that cause for which they gave the last full measure of devotion—that we here highly resolve that these dead shall not have died in vain, that this nation under God shall have a new birth of freedom, and that government of the people, by the people, for the people shall not perish from the earth."

After the Civil War, Jedidiah decided to make the military his career. He had been inspired by Abe Lincoln's speech in Gettysburg, and wanted to be a part of the Reconstruction, especially after his beloved President had been so cowardly assassinated on April 14, 1865.

He was sent to the Deep South after the war of brothers, where he watched with despair as slaves found their freedom but did not know what to do with it. Those that were freed by the 13th Amendment often found themselves arrested for vagrancy and placed on work farms. The county or local sheriff, who was rewarded handsomely, contracted out the labor that many ex-slaves provided to plantation owners. These new Black Codes and the overall mistreatment of the newest citizens of the country appalled the young soldier. Jed wrote in his journal, *"The lot of the black man is worse in many ways than when he was considered property."* Jedidiah was so frustrated with the politics and limited intervention of the military that he volunteered for reassignment.

Sergeant Montgomery was then assigned a post on the Western frontier, where the enemy was the red man. Jed had learned from the beloved Captain Sutherland that people were basically the same regardless of the color of their skin. Here he found a gentle people living off the land. The Indians could not understand the ways of the white man. Agreements signed by these two peoples were rarely honored by the United States; Jed knew in his heart that what his country was doing in the Wild West was wrong.

The repercussions of the many breached contracts manifested on June 25, 1876, as Jed and his men, under the command of Major Marcus Reno, battled the Sioux on the hilltop of the Little Big Horn. Outnumbered and in distress, the U.S. Military fought courageously until reinforcements arrived from a retreating Captain Frederick Benteen and his forces. Jed had survived the battle without injury, but he was heartsick at the slaughter and decided he could not continue with his military career. Washington's political heads decided to take a hard line to avenge the death of General Custer, taking a course of action that included the "total elimination of the red man problem." So when he was up for reenlistment, Jed declined, and headed south to Texas. Once there he signed on to run cattle to the Kansas stockyards in Baxter Springs.

Jedidiah liked being a cowboy, and it gave him plenty of time to think about where he had been and what he had learned along the way. He always carried a pencil and paper, writing about everything he felt, saw, and learned along the way. He thought about finding a woman, someone who would make him feel love as strongly as Captain Sutherland had felt about the lovely Sarah Elizabeth McKee.

I'm content here under the dark western sky
Listening from my saddle to the lone wolf's cry,
My bloody past is like a very bad dream

As I'm movin' these cattle beyond the stream.
The one thing I'm missing as the sun sets low
Is the love of a woman I've yet to know.

After almost seven years in the saddle, Jed was looking for new horizons and hoping something different would present itself. While in Baxter Springs, after delivering the herd to the stockyard market, he decided to get a drink at the local saloon, which had long become a tradition after traveling the long, dusty trail. The tavern was noisy and full of smoke from hand-rolled cigarettes and cheap cigars. A piano player was plucking out a melody as one of the saloon girls sang a popular song of the day. Parched strangers were ordering a concoction known as "Red Eye," made from pure alcohol, burnt sugar, and a touch of chewing tobacco. It had a kick strong enough to knock a cowboy off his bar stool.

Jed made his way to the solid oak bar and ordered a whiskey. As he swallowed down his drink, a fight erupted close by. Normally, he would have just moved to a different part of the room, but this time he found himself somehow in the middle of it. Jed was basically a quiet man, but he was never a man to back down from a fight. So, as the two cowboys turned to harass him, he made it clear how he felt about it, "You boys need to settle down in here, right now. I don't think you want trouble."

Their response to this was to give him a stare that looked like death was coming soon. The taller of the two said, "I think this cowboy is lookin' to die."

Jed had spent almost his whole life with a gun in his hand, and was faster than most. A hush came over the saloon as the men waited for the oncoming encounter, and saloon regulars ducked to get out of the way of any stray bullets. Jed searched the eyes of the two men and determined that only the tall one was willing to die.

The seconds moved ever so slowly as Jed read the intended move on the bad man's face, even before his hand registered the thought. Jed's gun fired on the troublemaker's hand as it made contact with his revolver. Then another shot rang out as the hat of the other troublemaker flew from his head.

Jed stared down the two and said firmly, "Okay, boys, it's time to go. Stop by the doc's place and see about that hand." With that, the two men quietly slunk out of the saloon, got on their horses, and rode away.

The town marshal, hearing the shots, walked past the two strangers as they exited the noisy bar and unhitched their horses. Marshal Kennedy moved through the swinging doors and asked, "What's been going on, Travis?"

The bartender recounted the incident and pointed to Jed, who had found a quiet corner under the staircase. The lawman moved slowly toward Jed and looked him over for a long time without speaking. Then he pulled a chair under himself and removed the toothpick from his mouth. Jed looked up without saying a word. When the marshal finally spoke, he smiled, "What's your name, fella?"

The marshal's badge was in clear view for Jed to see. He answered, "Jedidiah Montgomery."

There was another moment of silence. "Do you think you'd like a job?" The marshal asked, his weather-wrinkled eyes smiling.

Jed thought about another season of riding the dusty trail, sleeping in the rain, and the constant smell of cow dung, then replied, "Don't mind if I do."

The peace officer put out his hand and introduced himself, "Name's George Kennedy, but most folks call me G. L."

The two men got along very well. Together they made the town a better place to live. Marshal G. L. Kennedy was already in his fifties when he invited Jed

Montgomery to be a part of his team. His deputy's reputation of lightning speed with a six-shooter created a calmer atmosphere in the cattle town, and the communities in Cherokee County.

The local schoolteacher, Mary Jane Wilson, also noticed the change that had taken place since the handsome deputy came to town. She made every effort to get his attention, making it a point to be at the country dry goods store each time he made his rounds through the city. Before long, she approached Jed and introduced herself. He knew she was interested and quietly assured her he felt the same way. There was something warm and comforting about Mary, and Jed began courting her soon after they met.

In no time at all, the two were married. They bought a small cottage on the edge of town, where Mary spent every afternoon sewing and baking and making it a home. Mary loved cooking for her new husband.

In the evening the couple would sit on their front porch. Jed would tell detailed stories of his many exciting adventures, and every so often he mentioned his hero, Captain Sutherland. His description of Huntington and all its interesting characters made Mary feel as if she were there. Mary suggested that her husband write down his stories. He always responded the same way, "One day, Mary, one day."

Then one late afternoon as they sat in their parlor after dinner, Mary said, "You'll soon have new stories to tell, my darling." Then she smiled her special smile.

Jed looked confused. "What are you talking about, Mary?"

She just raised her eyebrow and placed her hands on her stomach.

"Oh, my Lord!" he bellowed. ***"A BABY?"*** She nodded. "A BABY!" he screamed as he danced a jig around the room. Then he fell to his knees in front of her, kissed her belly, looked up at her and declared, "I love you, Mary Jane Montgomery, with all my heart." He rested his head against her tummy as she stroked his hair. His voice quietly repeated, "A baby ... now that is something ... really something."

After the birth of his son, Jed started to contemplate the best place to raise his child. He began to talk to Mary about their options. He told her about the recent exodus of families from Baxter Springs, over the past few months. Mary knew what her husband was trying to tell her before his words could come out. She made it easy for him by saying abruptly, "Why not Huntington? If you ever plan to write about the Captain, then your hometown is where you'll do it." Then again she smiled her special smile.

Jed responded, "That would be a wonderful thing ... that really would be something." It would be another year before they were ready to leave Baxter Springs, Kansas.

* * *

Mary was tapping her husband's shoulder, saying, "Where have you been, Mr. Montgomery? I thought I'd lost you."

Jed was jolted back to the present as their carriage arrived at the hotel. He hugged his wife and child as he helped them down, grateful that he had been blessed with them both.

Jed wasted no time at all in securing a job as a policeman. He took his savings and set up his family on a nice farm on the outskirts of town. Jed had done well over the years, and that made the move easier for Mary.

Mary kept herself busy painting and decorating their new home. Handmade curtains done in gingham and lace made their parlor come to life, while wallpaper hung with the help of her husband, lent warmth to their home. The kitchen was Mary's main room, and it had the heady scent of fresh-baked cornbread as one day Mary appeared in the doorway, wiping flour from her face. She said, "Jed, get the buggy ready. It's time to visit our neighbors."

Mary wasn't one to beat around the bush, and Jed knew by the way she said it that the cornbread wouldn't stay warm forever. So Jed hitched up the rig, and they set out to visit the adjoining farms. The neighbors to the east of their farm were kind country people, and Jed told Mary how much they reminded him of his own family. There was a hint of sadness in his voice as he recalled the news of his parents' death while he was away in the service.

He was feeling good about their decision to move back to the land of his roots as the wagon approached the farmhouse south of their spread. A lovely older woman stepped off her front porch just as the wagon came to a stop. She gently placed her hand over her eyes to reduce the glare of the afternoon sun.

Jed greeted her softly with a "Howdy." As the greeting passed his lips, he realized to whom he was speaking. "My God, Mary, its Sarah McKee," he whispered into his wife's ear as he helped her from the buggy. "Sarah? It's me, Jed Montgomery," he announced. Sarah looked at him harder as he approached. Jed continued to jog her memory. "You went to school with my older sister, Caroline ... Caroline Montgomery."

"Oh, land sakes alive, as I live and breathe, Jedidiah Montgomery ... where have you been all these years?" Sarah exclaimed as she ran to open the gate. She embraced him softly and kissed his cheek. Jed thought to himself, "She smells of lilac, just like the Captain described her."

He introduced his family, "Sarah, this is my wife Mary, and my son Daniel."

On hearing the boy's name, Sarah slowly knelt down and hugged the child extra tight. She rose and invited them in. "Please come in for some coffee, and I just made some sweet cakes."

Sarah had them sit in the parlor and then disappeared for a few minutes to make the coffee. The room was beautifully decorated with rich imported mahogany furniture. Jed thought to himself, "Thomas gave her the very best."

When Sarah reentered the room, she said, "I'm sorry you couldn't make it back for your sister's funeral. The pneumonia took fifteen townsfolk that year. My goodness … that must be close to seventeen years ago." Sarah shook her head and then said, "Mary, I must tell you about your husband when he was just a tike." They spoke for almost an hour as Sarah shared stories with Mary about the young Jed that she remembered. "He was quite a rascal, and couldn't ever leave Daniel alone when he would come to town with me." She turned to Jed. "Daniel told me he thought you were very special, and that he hoped one day we might have a son just like you."

Jed smiled at her words and then gave Sarah an abbreviated version of his many travels and adventures, which had the beautiful Sarah on the edge of her seat.

Then Sarah spoke of her husband's recent death, "You remember Thomas Paine, don't you, Jed?" They gave their condolences. Sarah thanked them and then quickly changed the subject. "Your son is beautiful," she commented sincerely.

Jed couldn't keep back his desire to bring up the topic so close to his heart. "You know, I named him after the Captain." He watched her face for a reaction.

Sarah remembered the man she loved, and said, "Did you ever see Daniel during the war?"

Jed proceeded, "I served under him at Gettysburg. I was with him until the very end." Jed could see by her face that she wished to know more, so he elaborated. "When we arrived at the camp on the outskirts of Gettysburg, I was shocked to see Captain Daniel standing there with his leg all bandaged."

"Oh, my God! Had he been wounded?" Sarah said, holding her face with her hands.

"Yes ma'am," he told her as he continued. "I said, 'Captain, we all thought you were dead!' Then the first thing he did was worry about you, Sarah. He said he couldn't imagine what you must be going through." Tears filled her eyes when he told her that. Then Jed said, "I told him that you had married Thomas Paine, and how Thomas was there for you ..."

Sarah gasped before he could finish his sentence. She became very agitated as she stood and began to pace in front of them. "Daniel knew I was married before his death? Oh my, no! Oh no ... no ... no!" she kept repeating.

Jed tried to explain, "He made me tell him ... He needed to know you were all right after receiving the news of his death."

Sarah was frantic. The couple watched as she walked back and forth, mumbling incoherently under her breath. Mary grabbed Jed's sleeve, indicating that he had said too much.

Sarah thought to herself, "What Daniel must have thought on hearing that, after such a short time. How my beloved must have questioned my devotion to him. Did he lose all hope? Did I indirectly cause his death?" The images were too much for her to handle. Then she suddenly realized she was not alone in the room. She apologized and tried to regain her composure.

Jed could see that his words had set her off, and although his inclination was to probe further, he resisted. "Sarah, I didn't mean to upset you."

"No, no, Jed. I just still miss him after all these years," she replied, much more in control.

"Well, Miss Sarah, we really should be getting home," Mary said, after a moment of silence. She picked up little Daniel as they made their way to the carriage outside.

Jed turned to Sarah and said, "I hope you don't mind, but I would like to stop by every now and then to see if you need anything—repairs, goods from town, whatever."

Sarah said, "That would be very nice, Jed."

They waved as they headed back to their new home. Mary proceeded to question her husband about what he could have been thinking, "Jedidiah Montgomery, why did you put that poor woman through such distressing memories?"

Jed replied softly as he kept his eyes on the road, "I think there is more to this story than I had imagined. And it's somewhere deep inside Sarah McKee Paine and, darling, I aim to find it."

As the weeks went by, Jed made himself a regular visitor to the Paine farm. He would bring Sarah supplies from town and fix whatever needed fixing.

The conversations began to move towards Daniel and Shelton before the war. Sarah was relieved to be able to express openly what she had kept private for so many years. Jed told her that he would love to write about his hero, and said he could sure use her help in making it as personal as possible. She was thrilled to help him. So Jed brought his note pad and four or five pencils to scribble down everything Sarah had to tell him.

After a month of reminiscing with her, Jed was feeling that he now had enough material to work with, and he thanked Sarah on their last get-together.

However, she looked at him with her piercing eyes and said, "There are a few more things you should hear."

Jed was perplexed, for he had heard how Daniel saved his friend Thomas as a boy, how much she loved Daniel, and how Thomas came to console her after the news of Daniel's death. "What else could there be," he thought?

Sarah became solemn as she stared into Jedidiah's face. "I must now begin to reveal Thomas Paine's deception." Jed listened sadly as Sarah described how love could turn a good man into a monster; how his love for her made him falsely place her beloved Daniel's name on the list of the many who had been killed in action. What he had done to ensure that all communication between them would come to an end was still beyond her understanding. Jed merely stared, as Sarah described her late husband's dishonesty. She concluded, "I only came to know all of this on the day Thomas died."

Jed stared straight ahead, tormented by the revelation, and said in anguish, "I ... I was the messenger of his treachery."

"I'm afraid so, Jedidiah," she responded with melancholy. Then Sarah revealed her long held secret to Jed. "What Thomas did not know even to his death was that the child I carried in my womb was not his, but my Daniel's. It was for this reason that I married so quickly, for had I delayed, evidence of my condition would have been obvious. Daniel never knew he was a father, and he went to his grave not knowing for sure how much I loved him."

Jed looked at Sarah and groaned a heavy sigh of understanding. Then Sarah said, "You have in the words you've written the recollections of a man you looked up to and admired, and a description of the man I loved with all my heart. What are missing are the feelings of the man himself." With that she got up, went into the other room, and came back with the rusty old strong box. She placed it carefully on the table as if fine crystal was contained within. She unlocked the box and said, "Meet my beloved Daniel."

Jed went through one letter after another. Halfway into the fourth letter, he was unable to contain himself as tears flowed freely from his rugged face. He stopped reading as darkness approached; he knew he needed some time to review all that had transpired the past few hours. Once able to speak, he made arrangements with Sarah to return the following day. He gave her a hug and broke down again in her arms. Sarah held him like a child as silent tears fell from her face to the wooden floor.

Mary was beginning to worry about her husband when she heard the wagon arriving. When Jed made his way through the door; he grabbed his wife tightly and told her how much he loved her. He began to sob as he told her this again and again. She was confused, but she understood that something important had happened and that he would tell her when he could get his thoughts together. They ate dinner with very few words.

After little Daniel was down for the night, Jed sat close to his wife and shared the revelations of the day. Mary gasped at his disclosure and the couple held each other in mutual comfort.

His last day with Sarah and the letters was a hard one for Jedidiah. His emotions were running amok as he read his way through the last correspondence. He turned to Sarah and said, "How can I capture such love, such devotion? I cannot do him, or you, justice."

"Jed," she replied, "I don't know for sure why you came back when you did. I don't know why I felt compelled to divulge everything to you. I only know that some good must come of this. It just has to."

Jed went home and had a long talk with his Mary. She looked at him intensely. "Your story has only to touch one heart to be of value, and since it has already touched yours, its value is confirmed. So write, my darling, and never mind the rest."

With her encouragement, Jed spent the next six months typing words on paper until he was satisfied that he was finished. He handed the manuscript to Mary. She read while she cooked and cried, read while she cleaned and cried, read each night and cried, until three days had passed. When she was finished, she placed her hands over the closed pages, looked at her husband with tear-filled eyes, and said, "I should like to read this again and again."

Jed just smiled.

Chapter Ten

Samuel Paine looked into his antique hotel mirror as he began the ritual of dressing for the reenactment. He was to be a captain, and made sure all his buttons were polished to a brilliant brass shine. He was glad he had come to Gettysburg; it was just the diversion he needed to collect himself, think things over, and make some decisions. He thought about his last night at home and the argument that had finally found its way to the surface.

Sam had lived with Jenna Davenport for close to four years. They appeared to have much in common, with nothing really in common at all. They should have been the perfect couple, but Sam knew deep within his heart that she was not the one. His friends kept telling him how lucky he was to have a girl like Jenna. She had all the right credentials, and a pedigree to go with it. Blond, straight shoulder-length hair, and light brown eyes, along with a very attractive figure, made Jenna easy to look at. She had attended the best schools, obtaining her degree from Vassar, and she had hobnobbed with the rich and famous from New England's own elite roster of upper crust culture.

Samuel Paine was an up and coming journalist. He had met Jenna while doing a story on Connecticut politics and the future of the Democratic Party. She had spied him from across the room, and made her way close enough for him to get a good look. He got a very good look, and immediately decided to strike up a conversation with her. He made a casual comment about the young new senatorial candidate and his inability to put two coherent sentences together. To this she replied, "Oh my cousin isn't much of a speaker, but when he smiles, he lights up a room."

Samuel, completely flustered, quickly apologized. "I'm sorry I…"

But Jenna just giggled, and then she admitted, "He's not really my cousin." She waited for his face to drop in reaction to her teasing, and then boldly asked him, "Would you like to get some coffee or something?"

He didn't make it home that night, or the next night either. Jenna wanted him in her world, and made it ever so easy for him to move in and become a part of it. Samuel was foggy about his future, and Jenna was warm and comfortable, and made no demands—at least not at first.

As his writing began to receive more recognition, Samuel was given better stories to write about. When he finally acquired his own column, things began to change. He was often called out of town at a moment's notice to work on a story, or had to spend more than twenty-four hours on a lead that kept him from home. Jenna began to complain that he wasn't giving her enough attention.

On his return from one job, she mentioned that she ran into one of his friends, Jason Rogers, and that he had asked her to lunch, and how friendly he was. Then she added sarcastically, "I didn't think you'd mind if we had lunch together." When Sam appeared indifferent to her attempt to make him jealous, she became angry. "You don't seem to care who I go out with!"

The truth of the matter was that Sam really didn't care whom she went out with, and he supposed that it was becoming blatantly obvious.

The night before his departure for Gettysburg, everything came to a head. Jenna demanded he not go to the reenactment. He remarked impatiently while he packed, "Jen, you know I do this every year. It's just for four days." He then reminded her how very important it was to him. "I wouldn't even be here if it weren't for Captain Sutherland."

She screamed, "It's so stupid, and you only go to get away from me!"

"But I've asked you to go ... Come with me," he appealed.

"I would be bored stiff," she blurted out. She followed with an ultimatum; "Don't come back if you leave."

Sam felt himself getting angry, so he quietly finished packing his bags and placed them in his car. He returned to the apartment, looked her in the eye, and said, "If that's what you want, when I get back I'll pick up all my stuff and find a new apartment."

As he drove away, he fought off his resentment by thinking about where he was going, and why. Samuel thought about his family and the history that was America. He thought about his grandfather Joshua's stories of the Civil War and about the great Captain Sutherland. He had a damned good reason to go to Gettysburg and that was to represent this hero, his great-great-grandfather's best friend.

Sam looked one more time in the antique mirror. He had allowed himself too much time thinking about Jenna. "What am I doing with her?" He shook the thought off and went downstairs for a hearty breakfast of bacon and eggs in the hotel dining room. Immediately afterward he went briskly over to the barn at the edge of town to pick up his horse. The city kept a large number of horses strictly for the days of reenactment. He had been given a spirited steed with a dark brown coat and a black mane and tail. His only white marking was a star-shaped patch on his forehead.

The stable boy was preparing the horse for the temporary captain and had just finished saddling him as Sam arrived. The horse's name was Star, and Samuel thought the name was more than appropriate. He took hold of the reins as he headed for the location of his regiment. He liked walking a horse before riding so they could get to know each other. He reached into his pocket and produced two cubes of sugar, which he gave to an appreciative Star.

As he made his way through the township, he heard a lyrical voice calling, "Captain! Captain!"

He turned toward the voice and saw two beautiful women moving quickly in his direction. The one calling was waving as she made her way to him. She had strawberry blond hair and eyes that nearly took the wind from his sails. He thought to himself, "My God, she's beautiful."

"Where did you go? Jane and I have been calling for you all morning," Lindy said as they approached him. Samuel nodded a greeting to Jane as she caught up with the vision before him.

Lindy stopped just in front of the captain. She gave him a curious look as she commented, "What did you do to your beard?"

He could tell he was being mistaken for someone else. He said, "Well ... I'm just letting it grow out while I'm here."

At that, Lindy's mouth fell open and she stared at the handsome stranger. Then she poked him hard in the chest and, upon making contact, gasped.

Samuel looked at her frightened face. "You look as though you've seen a ghost."

Lindy just kept staring as Jane grabbed her by the arm and said to Sam, "I'm sorry. We thought you were someone else."

"Well, at least tell me your names," he said as they quickly moved down the street.

They were almost at a run, but they kept turning around to see him as he stood watching them. Sam was overwhelmed by a face of an angel that had found a place he wasn't even aware was within him.

The day couldn't hold Sam's interest, as his mind's eye kept seeing her face. He knew that face, and finally he made the connection. He had grown up with it on the picture wall of his mother's home. But who was she, and why did she call after him like she knew who he was? This was all pretty weird, and Sam knew he needed answers. As the day's activities concluded, he headed out to look for the two beautiful, ladies amidst a sea of strangers all dressed from a different era of American history, one of them hauntingly familiar.

The girls were just getting seated in a nice restaurant called the Blue Parrot Bistro, just across the square from the James Gettys Hotel. Abraham Lincoln, escorted by his team of security officers, had been taken to this hotel just prior to giving the Gettysburg Address, due to assassination threats he had received.

Sam stepped up to their table telling the waiter, "I'll be joining the ladies, with their approval." The waiter looked at both girls to be sure it would be all right with them. They nodded politely to the waiter, and then stared again at the handsome stranger with the scruffy half-grown beard. "Thank you," he said as he pulled up a chair. They nodded at the same time, their eyes glued to him as he sat down beside them.

After he sat down, Jane boldly asked with a bit of a drawl, "What might your name be, stranger?"

He smiled a broad smile and offered his hand. "Sam … Sam Paine."

Jane choked at hearing his name. Lindy took his hand and said, "Sorry about the confusion this morning. This is Jane McMullen, and I'm Lindy … Lindy Dennison. Pleased to meet you … Sam." She liked the way he shook hands, not limp but not too firm. The three guests made polite conversation while they ate, and Jane received at least four kicks under the table whenever she started to get too personal.

Finally Lindy and Jane excused themselves to go to the bathroom, where they discussed what they should do. "Jane," Lindy said, "maybe I watch too many *Lifetime* movies, but something became very clear to me at that dinner table."

"I thought the same thing," Jane chirped in.

"Really?" Lindy questioned.

"Yes, really!" Jane replied to her friend. "But how do we prove it?" she continued.

"I don't know, but we can't say anything unless we can confirm it," Lindy reminded Jane. Then she asked her friend, "Just to be sure we're talking about the same thing, what do you think is going on?"

Jane rolled her eyes and announced, "Sarah must have become pregnant with the Captain's baby before he was called to duty."

"Absolutely," replied Lindy. "Sam is a dead ringer for the Captain … Pardon the pun."

Lindy could scarcely contain her excitement. She had a plan, and she spelled it out to her friend, while Jane rubbed her sore shin.

When they arrived back at the table, another familiar face had appeared. "Jimmy Tortino, these are Lindy and Jane, my new friends," Sam introduced politely.

"Hi, Jimmy! We met earlier didn't we?" replied Jane looking fondly at her admirer.

Hearing the band start up, Lindy grabbed Sam's hand. "Let's dance." They moved to the dance floor and he pulled her close to him as the music played. ♫ *"You're just too good to be true … can't take my eyes off of you…♫ you'd be like heaven to touch, I want to hold you so much … ♪"*

Back at the table, Jane was trying to find out as much as she could about Sam from Jimmy Tortino, the curator ranger who mysteriously happened to be in the same restaurant as they were. He revealed early on that he knew Samuel Paine, apparently very well. She found out that the two men had met many years ago and were great friends. Once all her questions were answered, the table became quiet.

The silence was too much for Jimmy. He began to speak nervously, "Jane, the minute I saw you I thought I'd throw up, and I mean that in the good way. Since then I haven't been able to stop thinking about you. If you'll give me just a minute, I'd like to tell you about myself." He didn't give her a chance to answer as he took a deep breath and continued. "I'm the third son in a family of five sons, all very loud and very Italian. Our mom always taught us to speak from our hearts. She said never be afraid to say how you feel because hearts meant to be together will find each other, but only if they can hear each other coming." Jane sat with her mouth slightly open as Jimmy quickly went on. "I've been working here in Gettysburg for six years, and I've seen you the past four years. I know I should have said something long before now but, well, you're so beautiful. I should have listened to my mom! I knew I would just burst if I didn't at least let you know I think you're wonderful, and I'd love to get to know you better before you leave again." Jane sat speechless as he concluded, "So now, if you want me to leave—"

Jane broke in before he could finish his sentence, "Shut up, Jimmy, you had me with throw up. Let's dance." Jimmy was beaming as he escorted her to the dance floor.

Sam was having trouble talking as he and Lindy danced slowly around the room. His mind was reeling with the smell of her hair, and a smile that was slowly working its way into his heart. She talked about her job, her recent break-up, and how she was learning to let go and just relax. Sam finally managed to get in a few words about his being a journalist, but was content to hear her talk. He found her honesty refreshing. The contrast to Jenna was such that he thought about her momentarily. That thought cleared his head long enough to have him ask a few questions that were bothering him.

"Who was the Captain I reminded you of, Lindy?"

She hesitated, unsure of how to respond. She answered his question with a question, "Jane and I came across a CdV in the museum that belonged to a Captain Sutherland. Are you related to him?"

"You saw the CdV with the photo of my great-great grandmother. You sure resemble her!" he exclaimed.

"But how can you be related to the Captain?" she questioned again.

"I'm not, really. My great-great-grandmother Sarah McKee was in love with Captain Sutherland, and they had planned to get married when the war was over, but he was killed in a dramatic battle at the wheat field in Gettysburg, which is how my great-great-grandfather ended up marrying her. I come here I guess to honor his memory. My dad came here each year before he died, and so did his father before him. He said it was the right thing to do. It's our family tradition. You see, when Daniel was a young boy, he found my great-great-grandfather in the woods and literally saved his life, carrying him miles to the doctor in town.

But don't let me go on about my crazy family. Tell me more about yourself."

Sam looked at her intensely and smiled. For a moment she was motionless and smiled back, lost in his eyes. Lindy was beginning to realize that he didn't know anything at all about his real family history. But she did know she was enjoying Sam's company a lot.

"Well, I told you about my job and my cat," said Lindy, "and that about sums up my life these days. This trip has been the most interesting thing I've done in years," she continued as she rolled her eyes and secretly thought of her ghost. Then she looked into his eyes as she finished her thought, "And I must say—it's getting more interesting every minute."

They returned to the table, and as Sam pulled out her chair for her, he whispered into her ear, "I'd like to see you again, Lindy Dennison."

As she coyly brushed her hand against her cheek, she replied, "I think that would be nice, Captain Sutherl ..." she caught herself. "I mean Captain Paine."

"I'll be here for two more days ... how 'bout you?" he asked.

"Us, too. Jane lives in Long Island, New York, and has promised to give me the tour when we get back there. By the way, what happened to those two anyway?"

"I don't know, but if you'll allow me, I could escort you back to your hotel," Sam volunteered.

"That would be nice, Sam."

With that, the two got up and headed for the Trostle House. As they walked, they talked about what was important to them. They shared feelings that would normally be kept private, and both were surprised that they were revealing so much to someone they'd just met.

"You're easy to talk to, Lindy," Sam confessed with a warm and tender smile.

Lindy gazed at him. Then for the first time in her life, she felt a nest of butterflies trying to escape her stomach. She started to get dizzy, too. Sam could tell that something was happening between them, and as they arrived at the hotel door, he brought his hands to each side of her face and stared intensely into her crystal eyes as he moved to kiss her. In that moment, everything around her seemed to melt away as she was transported somewhere else. Their lips met. It was soft and hard, moist and warm, gentle and firm. It was the kiss she had dreamed about all her life. It was the kiss she was sure was only a fairy tale, but it was happening. It was happening to her, and it was happening right now. She could barely control herself as she found herself trembling inside. Then, just as quickly, they were back at the door of the hotel.

"May I call on you tomorrow?" Sam asked softly, and then quickly added, "Better yet, would you and Jane like to watch our unit at the wheat field? We'll be reenacting that battle, and then afterwards we could spend the afternoon together."

Lindy took a moment to remember where she was, and then replied, "I'd better check with Jane, but that sounds great."

"Till tomorrow then," he said, as he took her hand and kissed it gently. Then he moved from the doorway, watching her every movement until she was safely inside the hotel.

As her key completed its task and Lindy entered her room, she was reeling with newly found emotions. She danced giddily around the room with her arms around herself. Lindy couldn't remember ever being as happy as she was, twirling near her bed.

Suddenly she turned and gasped, "Oh, my God!" For there on the floor, curled up in a fetal position, was a half-visible Captain. "What's wrong with you?" She asked gently as she knelt down next to him. His appearance had changed drastically. His face had a haunted look as if he were dying of malnutrition. "Captain, are you all right?" she asked, very concerned. But he could only shake his head.

Daniel was unable to speak. He had been that way since he exited Lindy's subconscious the night before. There were restrictions within his ghostly world, a lesson that he had now learned the hard way, and one that Timothy had warned him about. His ordeal with her subconscious had clearly taken its toll.

Lindy looked about the room, trying to think what she might do to help him. Realizing there was nothing she could do, she sat next to him and began to speak, "I'll stay right here with you … it will be all right".

She talked about the Captain's love for Sarah. "I think I'm beginning to understand about love. I mean the kind of love you shared with your Sarah. It encompasses all your thoughts, all your energy. Actually to tell you the truth, I think I may have just found it. It's wonderful, and yet in the midst of these feelings I find myself so very afraid ... I guess there are no guarantees that come with these feelings."

Lindy continued, "Captain maybe you can help me. Love is an emotion that can find its way into your life in an instant, but what do you say or do to make it last forever? Is there some magic thing you must do to make it stay like that first moment that it enters your heart? I have so many questions! Your love seems to have lasted beyond your mortal life—and yet you are in so much pain. Is the joy you knew so great that it's worth all this sorrow? These new feelings I have for this stranger are scary—and now that his lips are not touching mine, I question whether or not I want to risk being hurt like you."

The Captain looked at her, still unable to speak; these were the very questions that had haunted him for over a hundred years. These were the questions to which he had no answers, save one. He thought to himself, "If I could have avoided this fate by never knowing Sarah, would I?" The answer came in an instant. "I would live this kind of existence for a thousand lifetimes just to know our love for one moment." However, in his present state he was unable to relay this answer to her.

Lindy pulled the blanket off her bed and wrapped it around herself. She wanted to be close to him in case he needed her, but she was exhausted from thinking, and feeling and sleep soon overtook her.

Chapter Eleven

Jed Montgomery called to Mary as he exited his Model-T and ran hastily into the house with a very important letter, "Mary, come quickly! You won't believe what's arrived."

"Land sakes, Jed," she replied as she wiped her hands on her flour-dusted apron. "What is it that's got you so excited?"

"It's from Washington D.C. Listen to this:

Dear Mr. Montgomery,

You are cordially invited to attend the unveiling of the official memorial at Gettysburg, Pennsylvania for the 27th Connecticut Division.

After careful review of the information you provided this office, we will be adding the words "Beloved Captain" above the name of Captain Daniel Sutherland, and awarding him the highest recognition of valor, The Congressional Medal of Honor.

Thank you for all your assistance in this matter. The service will be July 4, 1910.

Sincerely Yours,
Secretary of the Interior
James Garfield"

"This news will mean almost as much to Sarah as the day your book got published, Jed," Mary said gently.

"I had better let her know, Mary," Jed replied.

"Well, then take her some of my chamomile tea. She's been having some stomach ailments of late," Mary said, as she went into the kitchen to get the tea. Mary then put some honeycomb in a mason jar, covered it, and instructed her husband to make sure Miss Sarah used it with her tea. Jed got back into his Model-T Ford and drove down the dusty dirt road to Sarah's farm.

Jed knocked on her door. He waited, and then knocked again.

Finally the door opened, and Sarah smiled, "Jed, come in, come in."

Jed hugged her lightly, as she had become frailer the past few years. Then he kissed her cheek. As always she smelled of lilacs.

"Sit, Miss Sarah, I've got some important news," Jed said, almost too excited to contain himself. Sarah sat back in her rocking chair, and he gave her the correspondence to read.

She smiled and rocked lightly as she handed the letter back to Jed. "You had better read it to me, Jed. These eyes are beginning to fade on me." As Jed read the news, Sarah began to cry. "Daniel would be so very proud at what you've done to honor him. You have been such a friend to both of us, Jedidiah."

Jed invited her to come with him to receive the medal. "The Captain would want you to be the one to receive it." But Sarah, now seventy-four, was moving slower than she used to.

"I don't think I'll be able to make the trip, Jed." She said.

"I understand, Miss Sarah," Jed reassured her.

"You will represent us proudly; I know it," she said lovingly.

"I do have something for you to take to my Daniel. Will you come by tomorrow, before you leave for Gettysburg?" she asked.

"Of course, I will," Jed replied. He told her he would be leaving on the train in two days, and that he would be sure to give her all the details of the ceremony upon his return. Finally he remembered. "I almost forgot your tea. Mary would have my head if I didn't make sure you had it! She said to use the honey, and that it would help your stomach problem."

"You have a real treasure in Mary, Jed." Sarah smiled as she brushed his cheek with her fingers.

The next morning, when he went back to Sarah's place and knocked gently on her door, he was greeted with a warm embrace. She told him to wait just a minute and went over to her desk drawer. She pulled out an envelope that had the word "Beloved" written on one side and sealing wax on the other. She placed it into his hand and said, "This needs to find its way to my Daniel. Please do your best." From Sarah's demeanor, Jed could tell that whatever she had written in the letter was very important. Her good friend took the correspondence, promising Sarah he would ensure its arrival to the right place.

As he made his way to the screen door, Sarah embraced him tightly and said, "Jedidiah, you have been my only confidant, and the keeper of my most intimate secrets. You wrote our beautiful love story and kept our secret out of it to protect my son. You have bestowed eternal honor on my Daniel through your intervention, and for that you have my undying love." She then kissed him softly on the cheek.

As he headed home, Jed placed his hand to his face as he was still feeling her lips on his cheek. He then reached into his coat, and pulled up the letter. He was curious of its contents, but then thought better of it, and dropped it securely back down into his coat pocket.

The rhythmic train ride to Gettysburg was filled with memories of best friends taken before their time. Jed was looking forward to the opportunity to say a final goodbye to his hero—a man he had only truly gotten to know long after he was gone. Jed also thought about his book. He wasn't altogether happy with what he had written, for the true details of the Captain and Sarah Elizabeth McKee were so compelling, but he was committed to preserving their honor. "Anyway," he concluded, "who would benefit from the truth now?" Jed left the question unanswered as the train pulled into the Gettysburg station.

The sunny morning of July 4, 1910, was filled with hustle, as photographers from as far away as Chicago had come to preserve images of the dedications of over forty different divisions, brigades, and companies. Jed was amazed at how the Forestry Service had preserved the battlefields, as well as lining all the service roads with monuments to fallen brothers from both sides of the war. It was Jed's first time back to the cemetery where so many of his comrades rested. He noticed the exceptional respect exhibited in the words and actions of the many people who had come to honor their dead brothers, fathers, and friends.

Jed stood proudly when the names of his unit were read aloud. Then the speaker began to honor his commander, describing, in detail, the battle that took his life. Suddenly, through misty eyes, he heard his name being called to the podium. He was surprised, but moved quickly toward the speaker.

As he reached the platform, he heard, "By order of the President of the United States, William Howard Taft, and the United States Congress, we present posthumously to the family of Captain Daniel Sutherland the Congressional Medal of Honor, for bravery above and beyond the call of duty."

Jed was moved to tears as he accepted the medal, which was displayed in a satin-lined velvet case. He was the only person able to represent the Captain's family, and he was honored to do so. He turned to the large crowd of photographers and spectators and said proudly, "It is my honor to accept this highest recognition of bravery for a man I have loved and respected all my life. He was a man who valued, and saw the good, in everyone. He was like a father figure to those of us under his command at Gettysburg, and he went far beyond the call of duty to protect us on that dreadful day. On behalf of his loved ones, I accept this honor reverently."

After the ceremony he slowly walked the battlefield, reliving that horrible, bloody day. He retraced his steps to the Trostle House to visit the room where his hero passed to Heaven, but the building was under renovation.

So instead, Jed stood outside the building and said a simple prayer. "Lord, watch over Captain Daniel Sutherland, and bring him peace."

Then he made his way to where all the artifacts and personal belongings had been catalogued and inventoried. He asked to be shown the personal effects of Captain Sutherland, and was escorted down a long, narrow hallway, vacant of any kind of decorative wall coverings. He entered a large room filled with small, medium, and large wooden boxes, all on shelves and in alphabetical order. He pulled out one of the larger cartons, carefully placing it on a table located in the center of the room.

"What will happen to all these personal possessions?" Jed asked the custodian.

"Our instructions are that they are to go back to the family of the deceased, when family can be identified by the articles. If they cannot be identified, or if a family donates the articles to the museum, they are to be stored here forever and, on occasion, displayed for the visitors to the museum," replied the keeper.

"As the only representative for the Sutherland belongings, I then, would like to donate them to your care. May I take a few moments to examine the contents before I go?" Jed asked respectfully.

The guardian of the boxes nodded, and Jed began to go through the letters with the familiar handwriting of Sarah McKee. He was curious that one bundle of letters was tied with a string and unopened, after looking more closely; Jed noticed that all had a single postmark date. "This is the handiwork of Thomas Paine," he frowned to himself. "Do you open the letters that are sealed?" he asked the guardian.

"No, sir, our instructions are to keep things just as they are. This is so that visitors to the museum will see things frozen in time, if you will," he informed Jed.

At hearing these words, Jed began to place all the articles back into the large wooden box. Watching the caretaker, he waited for him to look away, then pulled Sarah's letter from his coat pocket and quickly slipped it in the back of the letter bundle. He carefully placed the bundle underneath the other things and closed the carton. The caretaker picked it up and placed it back in its spot.

Jed sat staring into space as the man turned and asked, "Will there be anything else, sir?"

Jed told him no, then thanked him as they retraced their steps through the narrow hallway and back to the main museum area.

As the train made its way back to his home, Jed thought about all he would be able to tell Sarah, and how proud she would be on hearing it. He missed his Mary, too, and couldn't wait to put his arms around her again. There was so much on his mind; he wished he could tell the world everything he knew. He was lost in these thoughts when the conductor called out, "Shelton—next stop, Shelton."

Mary was waiting at the station, her arms waving as she made eye contact with the man she loved so very much. As soon as she was within reach, he lifted her off the ground swung her around, then hugged and kissed her.

He looked down and told her, "I love you so much ... there are no words."

She had tears in her eyes as she returned his kisses, saying, "I missed you so much."

Jed was telling her about the ceremony and the Medal of Honor when Mary grabbed his arm softly, her news could not wait a moment longer. "Jed, Miss Sarah passed away yesterday afternoon."

Stunned, Jed pulled Mary close to him. Emotion began getting the better of him. His tears silently fell from his face, as Mary went on describing that last day.

"She was feeling weak all over when I made my daily visit to her. I called the doctor and asked him to come as soon as he could. Sarah wanted to talk about you and the Captain, so I sat and listened. She asked me to thank you for all you had done for her. She also wanted you to know what it meant to her for you to go and represent the Captain at the ceremony in Gettysburg. Then she started talking about the Captain, and how lonely he must be. She told me that she would be waiting for him. Jed, I didn't understand, but I could see her eyes were getting dim."

"I got up and looked out the screen door. " 'The doc will be here shortly, Sarah,' I said. When I turned back around, she was gone. The doctor arrived and said he had been expecting this for some time and that he truly didn't know what was keeping her going so long."

Jed asked her what time it was when she died.

Mary replied, "About 3:00 PM."

Jed looked at Mary, "That's about the time I was placing her letter in the Captain's museum carton."

Mary asked, "Oh my ... what did the letter say?"

"I really don't know, Mary, but whatever it said, it must have been very important to Miss Sarah," Jed replied and then asked, "When is her service? I should speak to young Thomas Paine about it."

Jed picked up the phone and asked the operator to please ring Sarah Paine's house. Thomas answered after only one ring, and spoke with Jed for a few minutes.

When Jed hung up, he turned to Mary, who was just coming out of the kitchen with some hot tea and fresh cornbread. "He has asked me to say a few words at the gravesite. What can I say about her, Mary? How can I speak of this wonderful person without revealing the secrets I have come to know? How sad is it that her son will never know the truth of his heritage, or share in the pride of his father." He took the tea off the tray and slowly brought the hot brew to his lips.

Mary watched her dear husband for a moment. "You will find the right words, darling. You always do."

As they stood over the grave, Thomas Paine, Junior, thanked everyone for coming and then said, "My dear mother's friend, Jedidiah Montgomery, would like to say a few words about her."

He looked over at Jed, who then moved closer to the casket as he began to speak:

"My dear friends, today we must say goodbye to Sarah Elizabeth Paine, a soul who surely has already found her way to Heaven. She was a woman of unyielding honor and a forgiving nature. Do we ever truly understand another person? Perhaps not, but I spent a lot of time with Miss Sarah, and what I came away learning was that she was a pure heart, someone who always tried to see the best in people even when they let her down, someone who loved the father of her child beyond our understanding of the word love. Someone whose love of her child was her most important job in life and keeping him safe was all she thought about. Most importantly she was one who understood that our heavenly Father has a plan for all of us, even if we don't understand it. She will

forever be missed by her family and by me. Rest in peace, dearest Sarah."

Chapter Twelve

When Lindy opened her eyes, she was looking into the face of her ghostly roommate. His appearance had improved from the night before. She ran her hands through her hair then, trying to wake up, and remarked to the ghost, who was still exhausted and semi-translucent, "You're still not looking so well, Daniel."

The spirit smiled weakly at Lindy and said, "I was pretty worn out yesterday ... I'm very sorry."

"Oh, don't apologize. What happened to you? Are you okay now?"

"Yes, I think so ... I guess it was just a kind of temporary condition."

Lindy got up, headed for the bathroom, and told Daniel, "I may have some news for you today about Sarah."

"What kind of news?" he said, weakly moving closer to the bathroom door.

"Just a minute," she called out as the shower came on. "I need to freshen up and get dressed. I am supposed to meet Jane this morning ..." She yelled from the bathroom above the sound of the shower spray, "I've got a few ideas, but I'm still doing some research and I need to check a few things out first." She didn't want to say anything to get his hopes up. "Why don't you just hang out here for a while, and as soon as I have something conclusive, I'll rush right back here to tell you?"

"Are you sure there isn't anything I can do?" he inquired politely.

She assured him that this was something she needed to do alone. Once dressed, she telephoned Jane's room and, upon hearing her voice, said, "Are you up yet?"

Jane replied, "Yes, of course I'm up. I've been ready to go for an hour."

"Great," Lindy said excitedly. "I'll see you in five minutes at the dining room." Lindy turned toward the bed. The Captain had moved to his corner near the ceiling. Lindy looked up and asked, "Will you be all right till I get back?"

He looked down upon her beautiful face. "I shall await your return."

When the two girls met downstairs, Lindy could barely contain herself. She asked her best friend, "By the way, what happened to you and Jimmy last night?"

"Jimmy is one of a kind, a diamond in the rough," Jane said as she rolled her eyes dreamily, remembering the night before.

"Will he help us?" Lindy asked.

"I'm sure of it." With that the girls took off for the museum.

On the way Jane asked Lindy, "What about you and Sam?"

Lindy hesitated. "I don't know. He frightens me terribly. He could break my heart."

Jane could see the fear in her eyes. She knew what Lindy was talking about, but let the conversation drop. They were almost running in their 1800s attire, which wasn't easy to do. They arrived at the door of the museum to find Jimmy just unlocking it.

He saw Jane and dropped his keys. He said, "Hi, Jane." then bent over to pick them up and hit his head on the doorknob as he was getting up. That brought him down to his knees, at which point Jane leaned over, kissing and rubbing his head. "Oh, that must hurt, baby." She winked at Lindy."

He opened the door then, and the girls rushed to the glass case that held the Captain's things. They examined the articles carefully, but saw no clues to reinforce their theory.

Jimmy suggested they go to the reading area. On the way there, he asked them what they were up to. They weren't ready to reveal anything yet. They asked if he had brought the book he had mentioned. He reached into his pocket and pulled out a worn copy of *Beloved Captain*.

The girls sat down and began to read aloud the story they had heard from the Captain, as seen through the eyes of Jed Montgomery and the Captain's beautiful Sarah McKee. It was a wonderful love story with a tragic ending. The girls had no idea how the Captain died, and they sobbed on reading of his death. There was, however, nothing, not even an inference; about the illicit night the Captain so beautifully described that first day. Over four-and-a-half hours had gone by, and Jimmy had come by a number of times as he went about his duties.

When he saw them closing the book, he asked, "Did you find what you were looking for?"

The girls looked up, disappointment written on their faces. Lindy looked into Jimmy's eyes and said, "Actually we're mainly looking for information about Daniel Sutherland and his fiancée. "

Jimmy described a room downstairs that held the extra belongings. "It's got memorabilia and correspondence from many of the soldiers. I'm sure there's one box with Daniel's name on it. Funny—no one has ever asked to see any of his stuff before."

They looked at each other and said together, "Sarah's letters!" as they quickly got up and followed him down the narrow hallway into a room filled with boxes of different sizes.

He went over to a large carton marked "Sutherland, Daniel Capt.," picked it up, and carried it to the dusty table. He blew the dirt off the desk and then placed the aged box on the table. He opened it for the girls and told them, "You're not supposed to touch this stuff, so please be very careful, or it will be my—" He left out the word but pointed to his backside. Then he placed two chairs by the table. "I'll be back later … Please be careful."

Jane followed him to the door of the storage room and kissed him tenderly on the lips. His knees buckled slightly as he said weakly, "I'll be back soon."

The girls looked into the container and carefully removed the items spreading them out strategically on the small table. A brass belt buckle with "U.S.A." imprinted on it, a tarnished silver pocket watch, and a pair of reading glasses in a little case were among the items on top. These were followed by a number of loose letters. Upon examination, Lindy organized the loose letters in order, oldest first. Then she eased the first letter from its envelope, opened it slowly, and began to read the contents out loud to her friend.

My darling Daniel,

I write this letter with a prayer in my heart that you are safe from harm. I am aware, however, that each day is a challenge as I listen to the old men at the general store discussing the war. Thomas has agreed to come by and pick up my letters to you, and bring yours to me from the post office as they arrive. How very sweet of him. He loves you so, Daniel, and he has told me to pass along his regards and to stay safe. As I am sure your time to read these words is brief, I will share with you my heart. You know that my love for you is constant like the seasons. It has, also however, changed entirely since our last night together. I continue to tremble at this memory. I walk around each day as if you were beside me, I can still feel your caress all over. My only desire is to hold you again for real, and to never let you go again. Please be careful, my darling, and I will pray each day that this horrible war will end soon and you will come home to me.

Forever yours,
Sarah

The girls were in tears as they moved from one letter to the next. Each one was more affectionate than the one before, as Sarah exposed her feelings for the man of her dreams, and her anguish of not being able to hold him in her arms again.

Lindy looked at Jane. "I think I'm finally beginning to understand what true love is, and the pain of not having it close by."

Jane replied wistfully, "Yes—Johnny and I had this kind of love, and it was so wonderful it hurt."

They had finished reading the loose letters that had passed through the hands of the Captain when Jimmy popped his head through the door. "How are my favorite re-enactors doing in here?" He looked at their faces wrought with emotion then simply said, "I'll be back later." With that the door closed. The girls looked at each other and wiped their eyes.

Next Lindy picked up a stack of letters wrapped in string. She turned to Jane as she gingerly untied the twine. "The return address shows that these are also from Sarah McKee, but they all have the same postmark date!"

Jane replied, "YES! This might be just what we're looking for!" As Lindy began opening them, closer examination showed that the letters were in chronological order, the oldest first.

The letters were becoming somewhat shorter and frantic as Sarah described the torment of not receiving any correspondence from the man she loved.

My dearest Daniel,

I am so concerned for you, my darling. If I could but hear from you, even just a note, to remove the horrible images I have conjured up in my mind. Thomas continues to come by each day, but he brings no news of you and no letters.

My prayers have become constant to our Heavenly Father that he will continue to protect you and bring you home to me.

Write soon!

Yours,

Sarah

One by one they moved through them, each one revealing more of Sarah's tormented soul, until finally they came to the last letter. This letter was different from the rest.

"How odd. This letter couldn't have been sent through the mail," Lindy commented to Jane. "It doesn't even have a postmark!"

Lindy carefully removed the sealing wax that had kept the letter unopened and began to read it aloud.

My Darling Daniel,

It is June 30, 1910, and I am sending this letter with Jed Montgomery to ensure that it is placed with all your possessions near your final resting place in Gettysburg.

"Oh my God! This letter was written way after Daniel's death," Lindy exclaimed. Jane nudged her friend and gently urged her to continue. Lindy resumed reading.

Jed is the only person who knows the truth and he has sworn to never divulge it. I have entrusted him with this letter in the hope that it will, somehow, find its way to you. My darling, there is so much to say to you I scarcely know where to begin.

First let me say that I love you as much this second as I did the last moment I saw you. You learned from Jed that we were told that you had died on the battlefield, but no matter what you might have thought in that horrible moment, my heart has never wavered. The story of your death that we received was a lie perpetrated by Thomas Paine in order that he might marry me in my grief. I'm sure you remember how Thomas looked at us when we were together. I knew he had feelings for me, but I couldn't believe he was capable of that kind of horrible treachery. He only confessed his betrayal of you on his deathbed. He had held all my correspondence to you, until the true notification of your death arrived, at which time he sent them all at once. This is why you didn't receive any letters during those last three months.

Before his death Thomas also told me that he had hidden your letters. He had placed them in a box under the floor of his office. It took me a long time before I had the strength to finally find and read them.

Daniel, your words are etched in my heart, and I have memorized them to give me comfort as my final days are fast approaching.

I have ached in my heart since I thought you were dead, and I didn't wish to go on but, my darling, something wonderful happened, for I discovered that you were living inside of me. I was with child—your child, my Daniel. My mother told me I must marry quickly for fear of what the townsfolk might say. It was all I had left *of you, and I knew I must carry on. Thomas never knew that the son he raised so proudly was your child and, my Daniel: your son is a good man. He is sturdy and dependable. He's so much like you in so many ways. He has become a farmer and loves the feel of dirt in his hands. He married a beautiful girl named Jenny, and they have made me a grandmother to our grandson, Joshua.*

You know that I have always trusted everything you have ever told me. It is for this reason that I am writing, because I know, my darling, that you could not leave for Heaven without me.

I pray that when this letter finds you and you understand the truth, you will be able to put the demons to rest, that in that instant you will come to find me, for I'll be by Heaven's gate.

Until Forever,

Your Sarah

Lindy and Jane wept openly as the letter ended. It was just as they had suspected, and it was just what they needed to give the Captain the answers he yearned for. Their emotions were running wild as Jimmy walked into the storeroom.

"What's happened to you two?" he questioned concerned.

Jane ran into his arms, needing a loving embrace.

Lindy got up abruptly. "We've got to go see the Captain, now!" Lindy ran past her friend through the storeroom door.

Jane kissed Jimmy as she followed her friend out of the room. "I'll fill you in later, babe. Don't touch anything!!"

Jimmy stood in the storeroom, happily stunned, repeating to himself, "Babe—she called me babe!"

As Lindy made her way through the door of the museum, Jane following close behind, they encountered and negotiated a parade of troops marching through the street. Lindy began to call out to the invisible Captain as she neared the Trostle House. She had no way of knowing if he could hear her or not, but she shouted his name anyway, hoping if he were nearby he would quickly make contact with them. Lindy unlocked her door calling, "Captain! Daniel!"

Hearing them enter, the Captain appeared in his corner of the ceiling, and made his way to where they stood. He could see that they were out of breath and excited.

"You've found something, haven't you?" he asked with his voice filled with anticipation.

Lindy told the Captain, "Yes, Daniel, we certainly have." She then began to reveal the story of a beloved Captain and the woman who loved him even beyond death. "You're here because you couldn't understand how it was possible for Sarah to marry so soon after the news of your death. And dear Captain, Sarah somehow *knew* you would react that way."

The Captain stared at Lindy as she reached into her pocket for Sarah's final letter and began to read it to him aloud. Ghostly tears fell as his friend's betrayal was finally exposed to him. Daniel had loved Thomas but he also understood a man's weakness in the face of beauty. A glow of light appeared on his face as he was told of his child.

As Lindy finished reading the letter, something very strange started to happen in the room. The ceiling began to glow with a bright light. Suddenly a sweet, tender voice called out, "Daniel!"

"Sarah!" Daniel said in astonishment as his eyes moved upward.

The girls could hear the soft young voice calling Daniel's name, "Daniel, my love, I'm here, I'm waiting for you!"

"Sarah, I've missed you so much, my darling."

Then Daniel and the girls heard the words he had written over a century before...

"Fear not your departure from this world my love ... for I will be beside you and I will catch you when you fall."

The girls stood speechless as Daniel began to glow and move upward in the room, his eyes fixed on his soul mate above him.

He looked down at the girls below him. "My most humble and heartfelt thanks to you both." Then the Captain looked at Lindy and smiled his answer to her question, "Love, however brief, even the pain of love, is worth it. Never let it pass you by." He then turned back to the light; his body seemed to become absorbed in it. His glow became brighter and then, in the next instant, he was gone.

The room returned to normal. The girls stood flabbergasted at the most incredible phenomenon they had ever encountered. They turned to each other in astonishment, but words could not find their way to the surface. They held each other in silence as they reacted tearfully to the Captain's departure.

Chapter Thirteen

The girls sat holding one another, teary-eyed for some time, still staring at the ceiling of Lindy's room. They were overwhelmed by what had just happened.

Jane turned to Lindy. "Love does finally triumph after all, doesn't it?"

"Yes, it does." Lindy then cradled her best friend's face with both hands and said, "We did it! We actually helped Daniel find Sarah." She was proud of what they had accomplished but also a little sad at the thought that she would never see the Captain again. They sat on Lindy's bed and talked about the experience for quite a while. After about an hour, Jane got up from the bed, remembering Jimmy waiting in the museum. Lindy also stood up and declared, "We will have to find Sam."

The day was moving quickly into night as Sam finally came across the girls making their way through downtown Gettysburg. "Lindy!" he called out as he made his way to where they were standing.

Sam noticed that Lindy had a strange look in her eyes as he approached her. Worried, he said softly, "What's wrong, Lindy?" Sam's voice brought her out of her trance.

"Sam! Hi, Sam. No, nothing's wrong." Lindy looked warmly into his eyes and smiled, wondering how to broach the subject.

Jane turned to her best friend and said, "I'll get back to Jimmy, as I'm sure you two have stuff to talk about." She raised her eyebrows, knowing her friend would get the message.

In that moment, Lindy knew she needed to find a way to tell Sam about his great-great-grandmother's life, and the truth about his family tree. She took Sam's hand as they began to stroll through town.

"I'm afraid we didn't make it to the reenactment today," she said apologetically.

"That's all right ... I was a little preoccupied myself," he replied with a small grin. "I'd like to talk about last night, because something happened to me," he continued.

She cut him off. "Sam, can it wait for now? I have something to show you, and it's very important."

"Umm, okay. What's so important?" he questioned curiously. Sam was becoming suspicious by the serious look on her face.

As they approached the museum, Lindy asked him to follow her inside. There they met up with Jimmy and Jane, who happened to be talking quietly in the corner of the rifle display area.

Sam could see that whatever had been said between the two of them had Jimmy somewhat unnerved. He was smiling uneasily as Lindy and Sam approached them.

Lindy asked softly. "Jimmy, could you take us back to the storage room?" He nodded, pulled out his keys, and led them down the long, narrow unadorned corridor.

Sam was feeling a bit uneasy, "What's this all about?" he asked the group.

Lindy squeezed his hand. "Wait, Sam—I'll tell you everything in just a few minutes." They followed Jimmy into the storeroom. The table still had Captain Sutherland's box on it, with the letters from Sarah Elizabeth McKee in plain view.

Lindy started by telling Sam about her encounter with the spirit of the handsome Captain Sutherland. He looked at her skeptically. "Sam, it was really Captain Daniel Sutherland, the same Captain you heard stories about from your grandfather, Joshua Paine," she assured him.

Jane confirmed what her friend was saying. "It's true, Sam. I saw him, too."

Lindy described the Captain's incredible sadness and restlessness as she recounted each detail of their encounters with the ghost. She told him about Sarah and the Captain's mutual devotion, and about his decision to leave her to defend the country he also loved.

Then Lindy pointed at the letters on the desk. "These are Sarah's letters to Captain Daniel Sutherland and Sam, it's really important that you read them."

Sam asked, "But why?"

Lindy sat him down in the chair at the desk, then moved behind him and put her hands on his broad shoulders. She rubbed his shoulders gently. "Please, Sam, do it for me."

Sam looked up at Lindy as he finished the first letter. "They were intimate," he said amazed.

She nodded, rubbed his shoulders again, and told him to continue. One by one he read the correspondence until he finished all of the letters on the table.

He turned to the group. "I never knew their love was so great."

Lindy then reached into her pocket and pulled out the final letter. "This is why I brought you here," she said as she handed him the aged communication from 1910.

He was appalled as he read about his great-great-grandfather's treacherous deed. Moments later, he gasped and put his hands to his head, as the truth of his heritage was finally exposed. He repeatedly wiped the tears welling up in his eyes as he completely finished the letter.

Lindy came around from behind his chair and sat next to him. She said, "Remember our first meeting? I thought you were *Daniel*. It's part of what motivated Jane and me to try and find out more information. Your great-great-grandfather Daniel Sutherland, had been stuck between Heaven and earth all this time, because he just couldn't understand how his Sarah could marry anyone else. It didn't make sense, because he knew Sarah better than anyone. So he couldn't leave … he needed answers."

Jane then added, "We believed that if we could help him resolve what was keeping him here, we might be able to help him find his way to Heaven."

Lindy continued, "When we found evidence for our suspicions, we took the letter to Daniel. The moment he heard the truth, something miraculous happened. The Heavens opened and Sarah was there, to take Daniel home with her. It was so beautiful, Sam." Lindy began to sob.

Sam looked at her, his own tears beginning to stream down his own face, for he had no words. She pulled his head to her breast, and then he began to weep in gasping sobs.

Jimmy left the room for a little while to give his friends privacy. When he returned, Sam slowly got up, pointing at the box, and asked his friend, "May I take these with me, Jim?"

Jimmy replied, "Regulations say that this is the property of the families. I'll recheck the policies, but I see no reason why not. Give me a day to get all the paperwork regarding release to family." With that, Jimmy put all the letters in the wooden box, placed a yellow tag on it with the name Samuel Paine, and put it back on the shelf.

As the group slowly walked back to the main floor of the museum, Jane said brightly, "Anyone for dinner?"

Jimmy responded quickly, "Just let me close this place up and I'll be ready."

Sam and Lindy didn't answer at first. Then Sam said quietly, "I think I'd like to just walk for awhile."

Lindy responded, "That sounds like a good idea."

As they exited the building, Jimmy told them, "We'll catch you guys tomorrow, okay?" He locked the doors, took

Jane by the arm, and they moved toward the downtown street.

Sam was still quiet as he and Lindy made their way toward the Trostle House. His head was aching with the incredible new information buzzing around inside his head.

Lindy looked at him. "Are you all right?"

"I don't know Lindy; it's a lot to take in. I'm not sure how to process all this. I mean my great-great-grandfather wasn't Thomas Paine at all!" He shook his head then turned back towards her. "The only thing I am sure of is that I'm glad I met you."

"I'm glad I met you too," she replied. "I have never walked like this with anyone and felt so ... so at home. It's very nice."

Sam, too, was feeling his heart come to life, but he was also feeling confused and unsure. There was Jenna, and that whole mess he had left behind just a few days ago. Yet next to him was Lindy—beautiful, warm, and sensitive. She looked up at him again, and at once he was spellbound. He turned and stood in front of her, brought his lips to hers and kissed her soft at first, then with more force as their mouths opened slightly. She reeled inside as each kiss brought another, until they were no longer in the street, but back at the Trostle House.

They slowly danced their way into Lindy's room. "Oh...Sam." She moaned as they found her bed. There were no words as they touched each other gently, just gestures of affection as they began to explore one another. His lips moved behind her ears as he held her strawberry blond hair in his hands. She responded with a mild moan and words that were inaudible to him. He began to lose control of his willpower. Her heart was beating faster than she could ever recall, and her stomach continued to spin as ecstasy replaced reason.

They were moving together as they began to release buttons and snaps. When he reached behind her to release her bra, it gave way without resistance. His hand sliding beneath the material found her firm breasts. His thumb brushed against her nipple and, just as this contact was made, Sam realized that he must stop before he was unable to do so. He pulled his hands away. Then he held her shoulders softly in a position where he could look into her beguiling blue eyes.

"Lindy," he said barely able to take a full breath. "I want you so much ... but I don't think this is the time or place, not for us."

Lindy's response was to close her eyes and try to reengage their lips, as she was ready to give herself to him.

He held her shoulders firmly and said, "Hang on a minute." Her eyes opened abruptly as he continued, "My feelings for you are stronger than I've ever felt for a woman before, but things are happening too fast. I want this thing between us to be right, if it is what I think it is."

"What do you think it is, Sam?" she whispered romantically to him.

He was hesitant to say what was really in his heart for fear that it was too early, and that she might not feel the same. What if, because of everything that had gone on, it was only a moment in time and fleeting at best? "I don't know what this is." He replied. Upon hearing his uncertainty, she sat up and angrily reattached her bra. "You're right. I wouldn't want this to damage you, for God's sake!"

There was hurt in her voice, and had it been anyone else she would have told him to get out and leave her alone. But Sam was different, very different, so she listened as he explained his hesitation. "I barely know you, Lindy, and yet I feel there's something very special between us. But I'm not in a position to take this to the next level. I have a situation at home that is not resolved completely, and it wouldn't be fair to you if I disregarded that for a night of pleasure."

Her anger gone, she looked at him admiring his integrity. She realized she wanted to know more about this stranger who was quickly stealing her heart. They talked all through the night, as Sam told Lindy about his relationship with Jenna and the feelings that were still unresolved in his heart. She shared her insecurities as well, telling him that he had brought out feelings she never knew she had. They never said love. Both were afraid to, at least for the moment, but the hours talking in the dark brought them even closer.

They had slept just briefly, as daybreak crept through the curtains of her room. Sam turned toward Lindy. "Good morning! Would you like some coffee?"

She opened her eyes, and then kissed him gently on the lips. "I'm glad you're here."

"Me too," he said, as he kissed her back.

The two got up, straightened their clothes, and went downstairs. Lindy couldn't stop her stomach from doing flips. Sam thought his stomach was growling for food, but then he thought again and knew it wasn't that.

They spent the day together, took his car and drove to the downtown area. Sam rented some bikes and the two pedaled around, talking about everything. Sam wanted to know more about the Captain she had gotten to know.

Lindy obliged him willingly. "The Captain was a kind spirit, who spoke about love like no man I've ever known."

They shared stories of the vacation spots both had visited at different times in the past. Lindy was amazed to find that they had been to a number of places within days of one another. They spoke of their hopes and dreams, almost forgetting to eat. When they did eat, most of the time they ate sparingly, lost in dialogue with one another, almost as if they knew their time together would soon come to an end.

Nightfall found them all too quickly as Sam drove Lindy back to the inn. He said, "I'll pick you up in about an hour, okay?"

Sam went back to his hotel to change clothes for the final dance of the reenactment week. He wanted to look just right for her. He mused to himself, "I can't remember ever being so concerned about the way I look." He smiled as he took one last look in the mirror. He jumped into his car and drove back to the Trostle House, where Lindy stood outside under the moonlight in a gorgeous red, period dress. The dress accented her small waist with the help of a hoop-slip, and really made her look like a vision from a time gone by. Sam, upon seeing her, almost drove into the bed and breakfast mailbox. He quickly got out of his car and opened the door for her. She smelled wonderful as he kissed her lightly on her cheek.

Upon arriving at the ball, Lindy couldn't help but notice the wonderful costumes on all the women who were apparently established reenactors. She was scanning the room when she saw her friend in a warm embrace with Jimmy on the dance floor. As the music came to an end, she observed the two departing out the side exit.

"I guess we won't be seeing any more of them tonight," she said to Sam as they found a table.

"Would you like a drink?" he asked her politely.

"That would be nice. Thank you, Captain," she responded in her own lyrical fashion.

After people watching and some small talk, Sam asked Lindy to dance. They made their way to the dance floor as a dark-haired, female singer on stage was singing, "♫ *Make believe it's your first time, leave your troubles behind,* ♪ *make believe it's your first time and I'll make believe it's mine ...* ♪"

After the dance they headed back to the room Sam was staying in. They were almost shaking as they sat on his bed. They began to speak about what would happen next.

"Sam, will we see each other again?"

"I hope so, Lindy," he answered her, sincerity in his green eyes.

Lindy felt the need to reveal more about herself. "There are things you should know about my past Sam— things that have prevented me from allowing anyone to get too close."

"It doesn't matter," he replied.

"It does, Sam; I want you to know everything about me … no secrets." He watched her face. Finally she said, "Here goes. My stepfather molested me. He told me everyone would hate me if I ever told. But I finally told my mother everything, and she went to the police and they arrested him. I've never told anyone about it, not even Jane. I guess I was ashamed. But I want you to know that I'm over it, and it will never again get in the way of my life and how I want to live it."

He held her tightly moved by her revelation. "You know that it's not your fault." She squeezed him back.

"I would never hurt you, Lindy."

There was a sense of urgency in their dialogue, as if precious time had been lost and they somehow had to make up for it. Finally, in the wee small hours of the night, sleep overtook them, their heads leaning slightly into each other where they had both fallen back against his overstuffed pillows.

The following morning, at about 6:30 A.M., Lindy got up and wrote Sam a note: In it she said,

Sam,

I know this isn't the best way to say goodbye. I really don't want to say goodbye at all, but Jane and I will be leaving this morning. You can call me anytime. My number is 760-555-5683, and my e-mail address is lindyd@cci.com

Please write me and let me know how things are going.

Lindy

Chapter Fourteen

Jane hadn't seen much of her friend since they were all at the museum. So as Lindy walked through the front door of the Trostle House that morning, Jane jumped up from the dining room table and embraced her friend.

"Where have you been for the past twenty-four hours, or should I guess?" Before Lindy could answer, Jane continued, "I think *I'm* going to move here!"

"What?" shrieked her best friend.

"That's right. Jimmy told me there's this great school here that really needs a history teacher, and to be honest I don't think I can stand to be away from the crazy Italian for a whole year. Gosh, I can't stand being away from him for even an hour. What about you, Lin?"

"Well, Jane, Sam's a really great person, and he makes me feel so, giddy inside. But he's got some unsettled business of the heart, if you know what I mean; anyway he lives on the other side of the country. I don't know what to think. We exchanged phone numbers and e-mail addresses, and I guess we'll just have to wait and see for now."

Lindy seemed changed from when they arrived. Jane couldn't put her finger on it, but something was definitely different.

Lindy went to her room and began to pack for the trip back to New York. She had gone through the room twice, and when she was satisfied that everything was back in her bags, she stood near the bed and looked into the corner of the ceiling.

"Captain, I've learned so much about love because of you. Now I know that true love is possible, and that settling for less is just not acceptable for me anymore. I understand the pain of saying goodbye to the one you love,

and the fear that you may never see each other again—I want it all, the good and the bad. *Captain, I want it all.* Thank you, dear Ghost."
Then Lindy got on her knees and looked to heaven.

"Dear Lord, Thank you for bringing Captain Sutherland into my life. I have learned so much from this amazing experience, and I will never forget it. Amen."

Jane was already in the car when Lindy made her way past the Shermans. "Thanks, folks! I'll be back, I promise." The old couple waved goodbye to the girls as they made their way down the driveway.

It had been one heck of a journey, Lindy thought, as Jane pulled out on to Harrisburg Road. The girls looked at each other and smiled as they settled in for the long drive. Suddenly they heard a horn sounding behind them. When they turned around, the girls saw two very handsome guys waving out their windows and yelling for them to pull over. Jane stopped on the side of the road and immediately jumped out, running into Jimmy's open arms.

"Call me when you get home, okay?" he said, as he hugged and kissed her.

Sam made his way to Lindy just as she opened the door. He leaned down and took her hand and said, "I'll be calling you a lot. Is that all right with you?"

"Of course it is, Sam," she replied, with her warmest smile.

He kissed her softly and then whispered in her ear, "Great smile, Lin. I'll be keeping it with me." With that he pointed to his head. He stood back up and headed for Jimmy's car.

Suddenly he turned as he heard a noise behind him. Lindy ran into his arms then jumped up and wrapped her legs around his waist. "Sam!" she said as she held his face in her hands. "I love you!" Then she kissed him hard on the lips, her hands still embracing his face. "I know it's real because holding you this minute is more important to me than breathing. I know you've got things to think about, but I couldn't let you leave without telling you. I love you with all my heart!"

She kissed him again, hard and deep. Jane, seeing that kiss honked the horn triumphantly. Lindy dropped back to the ground, but was there for only a second as Sam swooped her up and carried her like a groom, then deposited her back into her car, Lindy hanging on to him the whole way.

The boys went back to their car and watched as the girls got back on the roadway. Jane barely touched the gas pedal, looked at Lindy, and then both girls looked over their shoulders as the guys drove in the opposite direction back toward town. Jane then said, "Now there go two very sexy men." As Sam's car disappeared, Jane put the car in overdrive and made-up some time.

The girls spent the first part of their trip back to New York mainly just thinking about all that had happened. As Jane played the radio, the two let their minds wander back over their incredible week. Occasionally one would turn to the other and ask a question.

"Are you *really* thinking of moving to Gettysburg?" Lindy asked her best friend.

Jane gave her a pensive nod. Then Jane asked, "Do you think you'll see Sam again?"

Lindy could only shrug her shoulders with a small smile on her face. It was that way for the first half of the journey.

Lindy took over the driving at about the halfway mark, and as Jane fastened her seatbelt, she turned to Lindy. "I didn't tell you what happened last night. It kind of freaked me out at first, but the more I thought of it the more I saw it as a sign."

Curious Lindy asked what happened.

"Jimmy took me to dinner last night at one of the local nightclubs. He said that there was something he needed to tell me. I pressed him to just say it, but he insisted that we wait till after dinner. I excused myself to go to the restroom, and when I came out; I heard Jimmy's voice coming from a microphone. He said, "Jane, I want to tell you something with a song.""

Lindy's eyes got big as she gasped, "Just like Johnny?"

"Yes ... let me finish," Jane continued. "All of a sudden he started singing ... ♫ ... ♪ *'More than the greatest love ♪ the world has known ♫ this is the love I give to you alone, ♪ more than the simple words I try to say, ♪ I only live to love you more each day ♫ ...'*

Lindy, he could really sing—He sounded just like Bobby Darin! I could barely catch my breath, and then I started crying. When he finished, the place started cheering, and he came over to the table, sat next to me, and said that he had fallen for me four years ago on my first trip here, but had never had the nerve to introduce himself. He said that he decided that if he ever had the chance, what he just did on stage would be the perfect way to say, 'I love you.' The dummy will never know what his gesture meant to me. It was so beautiful." As she finished the story, tears were running down her face.

Lindy had started crying softly, too. Watching her friend being able to live again was the answer to her prayer.

By the time the girls arrived at Jane's house, it was early evening. Jane told her friend, "Drive a few more blocks, and we'll have dinner at my local Italian restaurant." They spent the rest of the evening discussing their upcoming visit to New York City, and both of them took every opportunity to bring up Jimmy and Sam.

The following morning, Jane and Lindy dressed lightly and got on the Long Island railroad headed for downtown Manhattan. Once there, the girls made their way to all the famous sights. First stop, of course, was Gray's Papaya, for the tastiest hot dog on the planet—a claim Lindy had to concede was true after tasting one. Once they had satisfied their stomachs, they took a cab to the theater district. Jane had a friend, Eddie Hancock, a stagehand at the Palace Theater, who had told her that anytime she was in town she should call and he would get her into the rehearsals for whatever show was coming out.

Once they exited the cab, Jane went over to a pay phone and dialed him up. "Eddie? It's Jane McMullen. I have a friend visiting from California. Is there anything good to see at your theater?"

Lindy couldn't hear what was being said. She saw Jane's eyes get very wide as she hung up the phone, then she ordered, "Follow me."

Within a few minutes the girls were at the stage door entrance to the Palace Theater, and Lindy was being introduced to Eddie. As he escorted them to a balcony seat, he instructed the girls to be very quiet. In the darkness they watched as Elton John and Tim Rice were offering insights into the music they had written for *Aida*, a love story that takes place during the time of the Egyptian pharaohs. The girls watched as the cast went over songs and the importance of phrasing emphasis. Two hours later the girls made their way back to the stage door and gave thank-you hugs to Eddie.

Jane looked at her watch. "Let's catch a taxi." She had no sooner put up her arm when a taxi pulled alongside the curb next to them.

"That's service!" Lindy commented as they entered the car.

"Twin Towers," Jane announced, and the car became a part of the moving traffic. Jane enjoyed showing off New York to her friend and knew that after what they had experienced in Gettysburg, this would be a welcome diversion. She watched her friend's face as they made their way up the elevator of the North Tower. She could sense that Lindy was thinking of Samuel Paine. They got off on the 107th floor. Jane announced, "Welcome to the Window of the World." The girls were taken to a table with an incredible view of New York City and a view of the state of New Jersey.

"Wow!" Lindy exclaimed. They sat, ordered a cocktail, and chatted about a time and place very different from the 1863 town they had just visited.

Lindy looked across to her friend and declared, "I am so in love, Jane, I want to stand on the top of this building and scream it to the entire planet!"

Jane smiled and said, "I'd better get some food into you soon." She knew even one drink on an empty stomach might be too much for her friend.

They concluded their day with a light dinner at a Manhattan Bistro, and then took the train back to Jane's house in Sayville. It was after eight when the girls arrived at the front door.

Lindy commented, "It's really nice out tonight."

"Would you like to go to the beach? It's just a few blocks." Jane's invitation sounded good, but Lindy admitted she was just too tired and would take a rain check.

Once inside, Lindy took a hot bath where she laid thinking of Sam. She ran her fingers across her lips remembering his kisses.

Jane knocked on the guest room door early the next morning. "Good morning!" she announced. Upon hearing a mild rustling behind the door, she went to the kitchen to start some coffee. She was peeking into the oven to see how her cinnamon rolls were coming along when she was poked, making her jump.

"Good morning back at ya," Lindy chirped as she sat down at the kitchen table. "The smell of cinnamon rolls is definitely a good reason to get up this early. What's on the agenda for today?"

Jane pulled the tray out of the oven and got ready to ice their breakfast. "I thought today would be a good day to go wine-tasting and check out the Hamptons. Perhaps we could have dinner out there."

"Sounds marvelous," the reply came, as Lindy moved next to her friend and stole a finger-full of icing from a newly decorated roll.

"Hey!" Jane cheerfully snapped at her best friend.

Lindy poured herself a cup of java and sat back down. She looked around the beautifully decorated kitchen. "Your home is wonderful, Jane."

"Thanks," she replied, as she brought the plate of fresh-baked pastries to the table.

After breakfast the girls got dressed and jumped into Jane's car, heading for the eastern section of Long Island. The scenery was breathtaking, with beautiful forests of maple, ash, and oak trees lining the Long Island expressway. Lindy put her head back as Jane's radio began to play!

♪ *Baby, you'll find ... There's only one love* ♫
yours and mine ♫ *... I've got so much love* ♪
and needing you so ♪ *My love for you*
I'll never let go ... I've got so much love

She thought about Sam going home to Jenna. Then she turned to Jane her voice plaintive, "Do you think I'll ever see him again?"

Jane took her right hand off the steering wheel and squeezed Lindy's hand. "I saw the way he looked at you. It's hard to ignore what I saw in his face. You spent a lot of time with him. What do you think?"

Lindy looked out her window. "I hope so." She continued to stare at the view that passed quickly by, and then turned to Jane. "The funny thing—more than wanting him, is wanting him to be happy ... even if it means being without me. Is that weird? I don't know how else to explain it."

"Oh, my God, you really are in love!" Jane exclaimed with a heavy sigh.

"I am," Lindy smiled. "And it's wonderful and painful at the same time."

The car pulled into a graveled driveway as Jane announced, "This is the best winery on the East Coast."

Lindy read the sign out loud and giggled. "Duck Walk Winery? Never heard of it." She looked at the sign again, which had white duck heads lined up in a row. "Well, I'm game," she punned unconsciously.

As they made their way through the ringing doorway Jane assured her friend, "I think you'll agree about this place, once you've sampled all their varieties."

The room had the fragrance of wine, and Lindy couldn't help but notice the display case filled with awards and medals for First Place and Second Place in regional and state contests. The room had clean, white walls and wood trim everywhere. In its center was a table filled with a variety of Duck Walk wines, and all around the periphery of the room were tables filled with gift baskets and wine paraphernalia. They quickly moved close to the bar to begin their liquid journey. An hour and a half later, Jane and Lindy were directing one of the vineyard workers to place the case of wine they had purchased in Jane's trunk.

Lindy tripped slightly on her way to the car and declared with a slur, "Best winery on the East Coast ... absolutely."

Jane started the car and headed farther east until they reached the beach area of the Hamptons. She parked the car, and the two got out and headed for Rogers Beach. Lindy, who was used to the beaches of Southern California, couldn't get over the tall grass that grew on the cool white sand dunes. They took off their sandals and made their way to the water's edge.

She commented to Jane that the water was warmer than the Pacific Ocean, "It's wonderful!" she said as they sauntered up the beach. Lindy turned to her friend and asked, "Do you really want to leave all this?"

Jane didn't even hesitate. "To be with him ... totally!"

"Totally! Now there's a word," Lindy laughed.

"It's a word I learned from the kids in school," Jane replied as she shrugged her shoulders.

They spent the afternoon walking along the beach, talking about life and the incredible turn of events that seemed to be sending them in directions they had never thought they would travel.

Dinner at Bostwick's put the final touch on their day. The restaurant was a wonderful place on Three Mile Harbor, with a sunset view from the second-floor terrace that allowed the girls to watch the small boats in the marina. It was a busy waterway, separating the shore from two small islands. The girls ate while they enjoyed the sight of the sun setting over the Northwest Woods.

The next day they went shopping at the local Sayville mall, enjoying each other's company. They milled around the downtown Sayville area, making their way home early that evening. Each was acutely aware that their visit was coming to an end.

"I'm going to miss you so much, Lin." Jane turned to her friend. "When will I see you again?"

"I guess we'll just have to see, maybe Gettysburg next year. I'm pretty unsure of everything right now," Lindy said. "One thing for sure, though: Whatever happens— you'll be the first to know."

Jane shook Lindy's hand. "The same goes for me, bud."

The next morning Jane fixed Lindy a hearty breakfast of bacon and eggs, toast and coffee, saying, "They won't feed you anything good on the plane."

Lindy walked across the kitchen and hugged her friend. "I love you."

"Don't make me cry; I've already put on my make-up," Jane said as she brought the dishes to the table.

On the way to the airport, Jane gave her friend firm instructions to call at least weekly with Sam reports, and she promised to do the same with Jimmy reports.

Lindy checked her baggage, then hugged her friend tightly. "You are my sister, and I love you with all my heart." As she headed toward the gate, she turned around one last time. "I'll call you when I touch down, okay?" Jane nodded and waved to Lindy until she was out of view.

Chapter Fifteen

Jason Rogers was an old friend of Sam's from their college days together. They had often dated the same girls at the same time. Sam never seemed to muster up much interest in any one girl, while Jason was interested in all of them.

Jason often joked that Sam was the only guy he knew who could go out with a girl for a month and never get involved emotionally.

Sam would immediately reply, "And you're the only guy I know who could go out with a different girl every week and fall in love with every one of them." Sam used to tell his friend, "Jay, one day my princess will come. I just haven't found her yet."

Jason had fallen for Jenna Davenport after meeting her at one of Sam's office parties. Jenna was a buyer for a department store chain, which was just a few blocks from the newspaper. Jason and Jenna spoke for some time before Sam approached them. "Jay, are you keeping my girl safe from the wolves around here?"

Jason had quickly replied, "Oh, was it my howling that brought you over here?" Jenna smiled at Jason as he graciously made his exit.

Just before Sam's trip to Gettysburg, Jenna had begun to realize that Sam was moving away from her emotionally. Besides finding him incredibly handsome, she absolutely hated to lose at anything. So when she ran into Jason one afternoon, after the office party, in Shelton, she began to flirt with him. She was hoping to provoke Sam into a fit of jealousy when he found out.

Jason was aware of what she was doing, but he had always had strong feelings for her, so he didn't mind the opportunity to spend some time with her. When he got back to his office, though, he immediately called Sam and asked what was going on between them?"

Sam admitted, "Well, we haven't been getting along all that well lately. Why do you ask?"

"Jenna just spent quite a bit of time flirting with me and I figured that something must be happening ... so I thought I'd give you a call and at least fill you in on her activities," Jason revealed to his friend.

"She doesn't want me to go to the reenactment, or go out of town for the paper. I think she figures if I stay in town, everything will be all right. But Jay, she *must* know we're drifting apart. I'm just not sure how to end it. Lately we spend more time arguing than anything else," Sam confessed to his buddy.

Jason didn't say anything for a minute. Then he disclosed to Sam that he felt strongly about Jenna, and he thought that she did, too.

Sam said knowingly, "I thought I saw that look on your face. So, do you think it's for real?"

"I don't know, but if you guys break up, do me a favor and let me know, okay? Jason hung up the phone, thinking of Jenna Davenport.

Sam had just returned home from Gettysburg to their apartment in Shelton, Connecticut. There were seven messages from Jenna. He was also surprised that his bags weren't packed. He felt sure that Jenna would follow through on her threat. He listened as her voice filled his head with confusion.

Beep—Sam, I'm sorry for being such a brat. I should be home soon, by Friday morning. We need to talk, I know.
Beep—If you check your messages, I'm so sorry for losing it that day. Call me when you can.

Beep—I love you. Hope you had a good time. Will you forgive me?

Beep—I was hoping you'd call. You didn't. Are you still mad at me?

Beep—I didn't think I'd be gone so long. My mother asked me to pick out drapes for her new dining room.

Beep—I love you, Sam … please call me.

Beep—I should be home Friday evening. Hope you're not still angry. I'm missing you a lot.

Sam's head was still reeling over his week away, but the familiar surroundings made his trip fade a little. He picked up the phone and called Jenna's cell. When she didn't pick up, he left her a message,

"Just wanted to let you know I'm back. Got the messages you left, and I think we need to talk when you get home. Give me a jingle when you get this."

He wanted to add, "I love you" mostly out of habit, but it just wouldn't come out. He wanted it to be more than a reflexive response; he wanted it to be real.

Lindy was beginning to feel like a dream to Sam. His surroundings verified that reality was back. He went to the kitchen and made himself a sandwich, then reached for the phone and dialed.

Sam checked in with *The Huntington Herald*. "Pam, it's me. Is *he* in?"

Pam, his boss's secretary, answered sweetly, "Hi, Sam. No, his wife came by and took him to lunch. That means he'll be a bear all afternoon. How was your trip this year?"

"It was more than I expected," he replied, thinking again of Lindy. "I didn't want to come home."

"Really ... that sounds very interesting," Pam said perceptively, her inquisitive nature piqued. Sam could tell she wanted all the details about Lindy. But he didn't want to get into it with her. So he asked for his boss's voice mail. He left a message, "Fred, I've got an idea for the column. I'd like to try something different, something outside the box. I'll be in tomorrow morning ... hope you missed me." He finished his snack and then proceeded to unload his suitcase.

He filled the hamper with his dirty clothes, and put away his toiletries. He then went down to the car to bring up the wooden box filled with the communication of two long ago lovers.

Needing to feel connected again with Gettysburg, he opened the box. He looked down in surprise, for there on top of the yellowed letters was the book, *Beloved Captain.* He picked it up and opened it to find a note from Lindy. He was pleasantly surprised, because it made her feel real again.

It read:

Dear Sam,

There is so much to say but now isn't the time. I will remember you always, no matter what happens. There is an unfinished story here and you should be the one to complete it.

Always, Lindy

Her handwriting made him smile. He opened the book and began to read. Jed Montgomery had woven his story well, making the young lovers come to life. Page after page Sam felt the love between the Captain and Sarah, while at the same time images of Lindy kept popping into his head. Sam hastily put the book down when he heard the lock on the door turn.

Jenna ran into his arms and kissed Sam hard. He returned the kiss as his arms moved around her waist.

She asked, "How was your trip?"

He began to selectively describe the events that had occurred. He described the weather, the battle reenactment, and meeting up with his Gettysburg friend Jimmy—but nothing of his new knowledge about his true heritage. And he discreetly left out anything to do with Lindy and Jane. Jenna listened attentively. Then she apologized for her immature behavior before his departure.

Sam went to Jenna's car, retrieved her bags, and brought them in. She put her arms around him again after he dropped the bags by the bed. He was feeling more at home, and he found himself reacting to her advances.

His inner self questioned, "Is this where my life is?" But then habit answered, "Jenna is what I've chosen." They fell into a loving embrace as all transgressions were temporarily forgotten. They made love until late into the night, when exhaustion and sleep swept over them.

The next morning Sam got up early and went down to the *Herald* where his boss, Fred Eversol, was impatiently waiting to discuss Sam's new idea. When Sam entered Fred's office, his boss blurted out, "Sam, what's wrong with your column? The only thing that needs a lift around here is my wife's face. Why do you need to try something other than politics?"

Sam responded somewhat sarcastically. "Yes, I had a wonderful trip. Thanks so much for asking, Boss."

Normally he would wait for some kind of tit for tat, but he had an idea he wanted to discuss and didn't feel like game playing. "I was thinking of a series of articles about love and all its complexities."

He had scarcely got the words out, when Fred jumped up and slammed the door, so the rest of the office wouldn't hear him. He then began screaming at the top of his lungs, "Have you gone out of your mind?" The whole office turned to the sound of his thundering voice.

"Wait a minute. Hear me out," Sam snapped back. "Why is it every time I have a great idea for a story I have to hear you go crazy, and then give me the standard *'Go hang yourself'* until I prove my instincts are right? I think my readers will grab onto this with both hands—which means they'll be holding on to your paper."

Fred bit down on his unlit cigar and said gruffly, "All right! Go hang yourself!"

Sam went through the boss's door, slamming it hard. He heard expletives from behind his back as he smiled his way to his desk and winked at Pam as he passed her desk. Sam loved to banter with his boss; Fred usually had blood vessels bulging in his neck by the time their conversations were over.

He stared at his computer screen, trying to think of an interesting angle for his column. "Love, love, love—what *about* love?" he thought to himself. The word brought images of Lindy Dennison and her kiss—a kiss he could still feel on his lips. Sam pulled out his wallet, and took out the slip of paper Lindy had given him. He put some tape on it, placing her phone number just above his monitor. Sam picked up the receiver, his fingers dialing the number as his stomach began to churn. The phone rang five times before he heard a sleepy, familiar voice.

"Umm ... hello?"

"Lindy?" A moment later he realized it was only 4:30 in California. "Oh gosh—I'm so sorry for calling this early!" Sam said apologetically.

Lindy's voice became clearer as she woke up. "It's so good to hear your voice, Sam. I miss you!"

"I miss you, too. Have you gone back to work yet?" Sam asked nervously.

"Actually I'm glad you called so early, because I go back today," Lindy said. "What's on your mind, Sam?" she asked with mild anticipation.

"Well," he said, "I've decided to start a series of articles about love, and I need an angle ... something that will grab the reader and make him think. And as I sat here thinking about love ... well, quite honestly, I thought of you. I uh ..."

Before he could finish his thought, Lindy cut him off abruptly. "How's Jenna?"

Sam understood the meaning; she didn't want him saying anything about them when he was still involved with someone else.

"She's fine. Thanks for asking," he replied with a sigh. "Anyhow, if something hits you about love, give me a call. I'll be here all day."

She answered with a lump in her throat, "Okay Sam. If I think of something, I'll call you back." She paused for a moment, not wanting the call to end. An idea occurred to her. "What about Kahlil Gibran? *The Prophet.* You know ... *'Think not you can direct the course of love, for love, if it finds you worthy, directs your course.'* The whole chapter on love speaks to the heart, and maybe it'll give you the hook you need."

"That sounds interesting, Lindy. I'll get right on it," Sam said gratefully.

There was a moment of silence, and then Lindy said, "Anyway, I'd better start getting ready for work, Sam. Thanks so much for calling. Call me back anytime, but preferably when I'm more awake ... Bye."

Her voice was lyrical as he heard the phone click off. "That sure didn't go well at least at first," he thought to himself. He had wanted to talk to her so badly that he hadn't even considered the time, let alone what he would say.

Sam sat for a while and thought about Lindy and her smile. "It was hard for her to say *I love you* by the car," he recalled to himself. Then he went to the Internet, pulled up "The Prophet," and went to the chapter on love. He read it over and over again, the words bringing him insight into his own heart.

> *Then said Almitra, "Speak to us of Love." And he raised his head and looked upon the people, and there fell a stillness upon them. And with a great voice he said: When love beckons to you, follow him, though his ways are hard and steep. And when his wings enfold you, yield to him, though the sword hidden among his pinions may wound you. And when he speaks to you, believe in him, though his voice may shatter your dreams as the north wind lays waste the garden. For even as love crowns you, so shall he crucify you. Even as he is for your growth, so is he for your pruning. Even as he ascends to your height and caresses your tenderest branches that quiver in the sun, so shall he descend to your roots and shake them in their clinging to the earth. Like sheaves of corn he gathers you unto himself. He threshes you to make you naked. He sifts you to free you from your husks. He grinds you to whiteness. He kneads you until you are pliant; and then he assigns you to his sacred fire, that you may become sacred bread for God's sacred feast. All these things shall love do unto you that you may know the secrets of your heart, and in that knowledge become a fragment of Life's heart. But if in your fear you would seek only love's peace and love's pleasure, then it is better for you that you cover your nakedness and pass out of love's threshing-floor, into the seasonless world where you shall laugh, but not all of your laughter, and weep, but not all of your tears. Love gives naught but itself*

and takes naught but from itself. Love possesses not nor would it be possessed; for love is sufficient unto love. When you love you should not say, "God is in my heart," but rather, "I am in the heart of God." And think not you can direct the course of love, for love, if it finds you worthy, directs your course. Love has no other desire but to fulfill itself. But if you love and must needs have desires, let these be your desires: To melt and be like a running brook that sings its melody to the night. To know the pain of too much tenderness. To be wounded by your own understanding of love; And to bleed willingly and joyfully. To wake at dawn with a winged heart and give thanks for another day of loving; To rest at the noon hour and meditate love's ecstasy; To return home at eventide with gratitude; And then to sleep with a prayer for the beloved in your heart and a song of praise upon your lips.

"What am I doing?" Sam questioned himself. "I'm not in love with Jenna. I've got to do something about this right now." He picked up the phone and said, "Pam, can you get classified to fax me up apartments for rent? Tell them to give me anything in the downtown area."

"What's going on, Sam?" Pam inquired with sincere concern.

"I met someone while I was in Gettysburg ... someone very special, and I can't keep fooling myself about Jenna."

Pam told Sam, "I'll get right on it, hon." A few minutes later his fax machine spilled out a list of seven new apartment listings in the area of his choice. He picked up the phone and made an appointment to see the best one on the list. Finally Sam called Jenna's cell and told her he would be home late and not to wait for dinner.

Jenna hung up the phone and cursed under her breath, "Damn him. Well, don't worry, Sam Paine; I won't be waiting for you. I'll just make other arrangements." She quickly dialed a number she had memorized, and said sweetly into the phone, "Hi, Jason, are you busy tonight?"

The response on the other end was, "No, of course not."

"It appears I'll be free to see you. Shall we meet at your place again?" She received an affirmative. "All right. See you at five, Jay."

Jason Rogers sat in his office thinking about Jenna, and then about Sam. He loved his friend and knew that Sam would never hurt anyone on purpose. So he dialed his old friend to let him know about Jenna's phone call. He needed to let Sam know that he was falling hard for Jenna and also that Jenna might not just be trying to make Sam jealous.

"Sam, its Jay. How are you doing?"

Sam replied, "I've been better, my friend. I think my princess has finally arrived but she lives across the United States and I'm still in a relationship with Jenna Davenport. I've got to end it now."

Jay wasn't really surprised. "Maybe I can help. Jenna just called me to meet her tonight for dinner at my place. She's still trying to make you jealous, I think."

"I know," Sam sighed.

"But I'm sure she likes me more than she wants to admit too. I've been holding off until you give me the green light. I wouldn't mess up your relationship for anything, and that's a fact."

"I know, Jay, and thanks." Sam hesitated and then felt the need to tell his friend more. "Her name's Lindy. I've never felt like this before about anyone, and I don't think I'll ever get this chance again."

There was a moment of silence, while Jason gathered his thoughts. "You want out, she hates to lose, and this is where I might be able to help," Jason said. "I love Jenna, Sam. I think she loves me too, but I won't know for sure unless I pursue it. Let me have this evening with her, and maybe you won't have to be the bad guy. If I'm right and she says she loves me. I'll tell her that I'll talk to you about it, and that I'll try and make you understand. Okay?"

"Thanks, Jay—thanks for being my best friend," Sam said appreciatively as he hung up the phone.

That night Jason met Jenna just as arranged. He told her he had made her a wonderful homemade dinner as he kissed her cheek at the door.

She said, surprised, "I didn't even know you could cook."

"There's a lot about me you don't know," he replied. She smiled as he lit the candles on the table. They made small talk during dinner, and Jenna complimented him on his culinary expertise. Then Jason looked her straight in the eyes and declared openly, "I think I'm falling in love with you, Jenna." He waited. The room was quiet. He wanted a confrontation. "Why are you here?" he challenged her.

"I didn't want to eat alone," she answered, too quickly.

"And I think you're a liar!" he said, raising his voice.

"Why are you angry?" she asked, bewildered at his sudden change in attitude.

"Am I just a place for you to go when you get angry at Sam?" Jason got up as he continued. "Well, I don't think so," he said more firmly. "You could go anywhere and be with anyone, if that was your goal. But you keep coming to me, and I believe it's because you have feelings for me, and you're too stubborn to admit it." Jenna stood up as if ready to leave. Jason grabbed her by her shoulders and brought his lips to hers. She struggled for an instant and then kissed him back with equal force. They eased into a warm, long embrace.

"I do love you, Jay ... I do ... I do." The words found their way past her lips as his kisses moved to her neck. He had wanted her for so long; the knowledge that her heart was his was all he had been waiting for. He led her to his bedroom as passion overcame reason.

Chapter Sixteen

The weeks had turned to months since Lindy got home. It had become apparent to her friends that something about her had changed. Something was definitely going on, but no one could put his or her finger on it—no one, that is, except Mrs. Miaorano. She had looked deeply into Lindy's eyes when she had come to pick up her cat, saying, "You are ina lova. I'ya can see it. You'a eyes, they are singin!"

Lindy knew the sweet old lady was right, but just smiled and said nothing. She never imagined the feelings that came with love would find their way into her heart, but they had. She was in love, and she wanted the world to know it. It was only her fear that Sam might not feel the same way that prevented her from broadcasting it.

That first call wasn't the best, but hearing his voice made it worthwhile. She started to worry when, after a few days had gone by, he hadn't called again. She considered calling him, but thought better of it. If he had things to think about, she didn't want to add to his confusion. He had to do this on his own; that much she was sure of.

When his next call came, Lindy had to grab her tummy when she heard his voice on the line. Sam told her he had moved out of Jenna's apartment and had gotten his own place. He relayed the story about his best friend and Jenna. Lindy became very excited. He talked about his work and about their time together. Then his voice became very serious. "I've been doing a lot of soul-searching. And the one thing I know for sure now, is that I love you, Lindy Dennison, and I thought you should know it as soon as I realized it."

"I love you too, Sam," she replied, as tears fell on the phone.

He told her he was missing her smile. The very next day she took a picture of herself and sent it via the e-mail. In it she was smiling, and the note said *"With all my Love, Lindy."*

After that, Sam either called or emailed every day, and Lindy emailed him back. With each communication he learned more about her, and even more about himself. He was sharing his heart for the first time, and it felt wonderful.

He called her, where she worked, to tell her the paper had finally released his first article on love. His boss decided to release it once a week, since the first one got such a big response. "I'm very proud of this article. We've already received a large number of calls from all over thanking us for coming up with something more personal than politics and the economy."

Lindy promised him she would read it as soon as she got home from work and then added, "I'll call you each week after I've read them … okay?"

That evening she ran to her desktop and pulled up the *Huntington Herald*. She scanned the articles and then found Sam's column. It read *About Love,* by Sam Paine.

> *I've been writing for the Herald for some time, and until recently I have had no difficulty in bringing you my take on what's going on locally and nationally, and how things could affect us in the long run. It was never hard to tell you how I felt about anything. But when I decided to write about LOVE, I had to search the depths of my being, and in doing so reveal more of myself. For the next few weeks, these articles will be very personal, but my hope is that they will make us all look deeply into ourselves and remember the glorious emotion that some of us take for granted— the feeling some of us let get away or worse the passion some of us have for someone and haven't*

told him or her. Love represents the best of us, and when we forget to show it ... everyone loses.

I'm learning to love again...
After yesterday's dreams were shattered and destroyed beyond recognition by those who envisioned security...
When there was nothing but self-doubt ...
Safety...when there was only danger ...
A straight path towards tomorrow...
When that road was full of detours that moved me in directions I never expected to travel.

I'm learning to love again ... to start anew.
Exposing myself one more time for that incredible opportunity to live again...
To imagine all the possibilities love might bring me for a while...
A moment to soar far above cirrus clouds...
A second to capture myself touching lips that will remain in my memory long after all else is forgotten
To feel the pain of too much love as it bursts beyond the confines of my soul...
To shed tears of ecstasy as eyes meet and the knowledge of what moves between us brings awareness of the infinite...
An instant when through her eyes I am in the sight of God...
This I am prepared to do...because I'm learning to love again...

Lindy could barely contain herself as she fumbled with the buttons on the phone. Sam answered after the second ring when he saw her number appear on his phone panel. "What did you think?"

"Oh, my goodness! You're a poet!" she exclaimed into the phone. "You never told me that when we were together."

Sam wasn't too good at accepting compliments but he mustered a mumbled, "Thank you, Lindy." Then quickly changed the subject, "How is work going?"

She answered with complete honesty, "It's hard to concentrate. I miss you so much it hurts! Now I know what it was like for Sarah each day as she waited for word from Daniel." Then she added, "But at least I can pick up the phone and talk to you every day. How did she do it? I don't know."

Sam surprised her when he said, "I don't know how you and I got so close so soon, but I've never felt so sure of anyone in my life. I find myself loving you more each day, and I don't understand how that's possible."

They talked for almost an hour about little things they liked and disliked, things they liked to do, and anything else they could think of so they wouldn't have to hang up the phone. This became a ritual each time another article made the paper. Each article began with a few personal words and then more poetry.

When love for someone becomes revealed and that person feels the same way too, it's magic! I have had the rare opportunity to get a first-hand look into the immense love of my own two great great grandparents, through the letters they sent back and forth to each other during the Civil War. True love goes beyond the moment or the day or even the year. When you love someone they become your world.

"There is Only You"
'When the lights go out ... there is only you.
When the stars light up the sky ... there is only you.
When the sun breaks through the rain clouds ...

there is only you.
When winter melts to spring ... there is only you.
When summer sun is blown to fall leaves ...
there is only you...
And when my life transcends this world ...
I'll smile one last smile for there will be ... only you!'

Fred Eversol hated being proven wrong, but he had to admit that his reporter was right again. His arms were filled with letters and faxes and phone messages from people all over the community; people who just wanted to say thank you for the articles, and to keep them coming. He dropped them on Pam's desk, then popped his head into Sam's cubical, and joked, "I guess the hanging will have to wait."

Lindy went on the Internet to read the articles each week, and each week she was brought to tears as she began to understand the heart of the man she loved. She pained to see him, and found herself singing with her stereo,
♪ *'Sam Sam, you know where I am;* ♫ *come around and talk awhile; I need your smile;* ♪ *you need a shoulder, oh, Sam ...* ♫ *...'*

At night Lindy squeezed her pillow and thought about his face, his touch, and his love, that was becoming clearer with each editorial. She pretended the pillow was Sam and tried to remember his smell as she cried herself to sleep.

"It's been just over four months since Sam and I had our last kiss, and the thought of going through the holidays without seeing each other just isn't acceptable," Lindy complained in her phone update, to Jane. Her friend suggested, "Just grab a flight out there."

"I wish it were that easy. I've had to do two trade shows in the past month, and my last one is this week. I'm hoping we can see each other right after Christmas."

"Hang in there, babe. It isn't that far away," Jane encouraged. They hung up, as Lindy was about to leave work for home.

The final commentary on love was waiting for her as Lindy kicked off her shoes on her way to the computer. She rubbed her eyes as the screen came up to its preset location. Lindy's jaw dropped as she stared at the screen in disbelief. It read, *About Love* by Samuel Sutherland. Lindy couldn't read anything as her eyes filled with tears; her fingers touched the screen trying hopelessly to make contact with Sam. She picked up her phone and called his cellular. It had rung only once when she heard his voice.

"Samuel Sutherland—can I help you?" There was laughter in his voice.

"Sam! Your name! When did you do this?"

"I read and reread the letters from my great-great-grandparents. They were so in love. If Thomas hadn't intervened I'd still be here, but my name would be Sutherland. I just felt that this would be my way of making things right," he told her in a voice filled with new conviction.

"This would make the Captain and Sarah so proud. Oh Sam, I love you so much."

"Well?" he questioned her.

"What?" she questioned back.

"The piece, what did you think?"

"I haven't read the article yet … I couldn't get past your name, and I just had to call you." She confessed.

"Well, I think you should read the article. I think it's the best of the series," Sam said proudly. "I'll call you back in a few minutes, okay?"

She said, "Okay!" and hung up the phone. Then she began to read,

> *'I've been writing for this paper for quite a few years, and most people know that love is not a topic*

*they've ever seen covered in my column. However, I
had to write this series, because I needed to
understand the new feelings that were becoming a
part of my life. I have never known love before. I had
reached a point in my life where I thought I might
never find it.*

*Then in an instant, on the streets of Gettysburg, it
arrived. Love wrapped itself around my virgin heart
and brought life to me, life, as I have never known it
before. Now, I wake each morning to the memory of
her smile. I find myself searching for her in the
crowds on city streets, where I know she won't be.
I'm sure I can smell her as I enter the elevator on my
way to work. I ache inside because she is not near
me. I can hear her tender voice almost like a song
as I try desperately to remember her every detail. I
love her and I know it, because her happiness has
become more important than the air I breathe. I can't
wait another moment to hold her in my arms again,
to kiss her lips that melt into mine, to tell her I love
her over and over and over again.*

*Could I but pick the second that my life began
again? It is not within my power, but I know the day.
A day that is so very clear in my memory that I relive
it moment to moment. You brought the hope that
happily ever after is possible. A life of sharing good
times, bad times, sickness and health warms my
soul. I cannot promise you wealth seen in the
purchases of the day, but if you treasure quiet walks
in the moonlight, and long warm caresses after
making love, you will be wealthy beyond words. If
being well off means to you that for the rest of your
life you can share your very being and know without
a doubt that the heart that lies next to you beats with
the same rhythm occasionally skipping a beat at the*

wonder of you. Then you will be well off. If being rich to you is a lifetime of security in the knowledge that you are loved ... because of who you are ... what you're made of ... what you believe in ... and everything that makes you ... you.
Then you will be the richest woman in the world...and I will be the luckiest man.
So, will you marry me, Lindy Dennison?

In that instant the phone rang and Lindy fumbled to pick it up. She knew it was her Sam on the other end. She shouted with joy, "Yes, Sam! Yes! Yes! Yes!"

Sam's voice returned quietly, "Then will you please open the door."

She stood in shock, motionless, until his words made their way into her consciousness, and then she ran to the door. "Sam!" she exclaimed, flinging the door open.

She jumped into his arms and kissed him all over his face. He held her off the ground as they spun together. He kissed her with short kisses at first, and then long and tenderly, until they both had to stop and catch their breath. They stared into each other's tear-filled eyes. Finally they giggled, "I love you" to each other over and over.

Lindy took Sam's face in both of her hands. "I've been waiting for you all my life."

The End

Something

There must be something about you I've missed
Although I can't think of what it is,
Something…
Something that isn't right
Something that I can't deal with
But I haven't found it yet…
It's always been so easy to do
With the others I've known…
Too much of this…
Too little of that…
But there's always been something,
Until now…

Taken from Learning to Love

Inspiration

In this hour of lost sleep and clouded thoughts
I have been inspired...
Not by the cascade of stars against the midnight blue...
Not by the music that echoes through my soul...
My inspiration is a whisper in white and I am humbled by
her.
For through her smile, I have found the freedom to write
again
Through her lips passes the wisdom of the world
Through her eyes I can see beyond sheets and blankets
A love that poets spend a lifetime describing.
So in this hour of lost sleep and clouded thoughts
I have been inspired...

Taken from Learning to Love Again

The Rainbow Chaser

They said that she could have been a Prima Ballerina,
But instead she chose to dance along a beam with her
arms extended gracefully
And swing unparalleled to the rhythm created in her mind...
She was but a child then,
With aspirations of triumphs and trophies
Filling her waking hours,
Dreams of Mt. Olympus, interwoven rings
And medals of gold, silver, and bronze.
She had become disciplined to the tasks at hand,
Following commands without question.
School to gym to bed...school to gym to bed...
Day after day...year after year.
Perfecting her art...
But...neglecting her heart...
Her small muscular body began to undergo
metamorphosis,
Her hard lines became soft curves.
Her desires and goals carried her to the place of
commitment
Where the arms that embraced her were nice arms...
And being untrained in matters of the heart,
She told herself, "This must be love!"

Excerpt from The Rainbow Chaser and other stories

About the Author

Philip N. Rogone has been writing since the age of sixteen, when his English teacher introduced him to poetry. His first published poem was the last page of the Damien High School yearbook 1970. At eighteen he entered the U.S. Army where he improved his prose skills by writing love letters for his Army buddies.

Philip has had his poetry published in different poetry periodicals like Poets at Work, over the years, but has only recently decided to release his works.

He did some theater work in San Diego in the seventies, and extra-work in Hollywood in the eighties. He has been many things in his lifetime including a laborer, a waiter, a cook, an auto battery salesman, a bartender, a restaurant manager, a toy store manager, a landscaper, a handyman, a janitor, an orderly, a respiratory therapist, a physician assistant, an inventor, and is currently the Director of Sales for a medical device manufacturer.

He has written three books of poetry using the pen name, *The Rogue,* two children's picture books, and is currently working on his second novel.

He has five sons, two stepsons, three stepdaughters, two granddaughters, and three grandsons. He loves them all. Most importantly, he has a wife who has taught him that the detour in life is the path, and that love can grow stronger with each and every passing year.

Please contact Mr. Rogone with comments, e-mail him at

apoetrogue@yahoo.com
Or go to
www.thegettysburgghost.com

To order any books by P.N. Rogone contact
Caring Creations Publishing at
www.caringcreations.com

POETRY
Learning to Love
The true story of a young boy's quest for love

The Rainbow Chaser and other
stories. A compilation of many poems

Learning to Love Again
Discovering love when you think it isn't possible anymore

PICTURE BOOKS

The Princess Frog
Artwork by Amber Sandlin and Johnny Rogone
A story of a princess frog that thinks she's missed
something and leaves her life to find more…

The Boy in the Mirror
Artwork by Amber Sandlin
A boy's journey to find the truth about himself.